W E
D R E A M
O F
W A T E R

Also by Srdjan Smajić

Ghost-Seers, Detectives, and Spiritualists: Theories of Vision in Victorian Literature and Science (Cambridge Studies in Nineteenth-Century Literature and Culture)

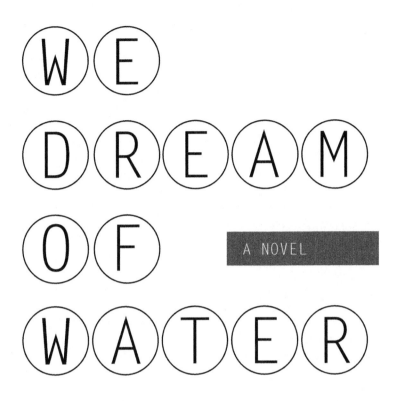

WE DREAM OF WATER

A NOVEL

SRDJAN SMAJIĆ

Underland Press

This is U019, and it has an ISBN of 978-1-63023-020-3.

This book was printed in the United States of America, and it is published by Underland Press, an imprint of Resurrection House (Puyallup, WA).

Lines and shadows.

Edited by Darin Bradley
Cover Design by Darin Bradley
Book Design by Aaron Leis

First Underland Press edition: October 2015.

www.resurrectionhouse.com

For Darin and Rima

WE DREAM OF WATER

1

Mick gets knifed coming home from his shift at Jack's, and Maggie calls me the next morning to tell me about it. He drove himself to the ER, she says, he lost a pint of blood on the way. They sewed him up and put him in a room, he's going to be okay.

"Jesus, Jimmy," she says. "Right outside his house."

The light hurts my eyes.

I raise my head enough to see I'm still in my clothes, still in my shoes.

I don't exactly well up with pride, but one thing less I have to do today is get dressed. It's a trick I'm trying to pick up, looking on the bright side. I'm starting to see results already, though I can't say it's doing much for my hygiene. I'm calling it a tradeoff.

"Are you even listening?" she says.

I cough and hack and bring up a wad of something ugly, a slithery lump that sits on my tongue.

"Jesus," she says. "What the fuck. You okay?"

I have nowhere to spit. I swallow.

"Top of the mountain," I say.

She's going to go see him at Touro, but she's out of a ride, her truck's in the shop, she needs me to drive her.

"Can't you take a bus?" I say. As in public transport? Am I insane? Have I been in one of those things? She'll catch AIDS or Ebola or something worse. What am I doing that I'm so goddamn busy anyway? I don't want to play chauffeur. What I want to do is smoke my morning cigarette and drink my coffee and take that shit I've been thinking about for the last two days, the one that's going to make everything all right again. I have big hopes for this one, great expectations.

"Fine," I say. "But you be there. You be on the street, I'm not coming up to fetch you. Thirty minutes."

Mick is what you'd call a natural asshole. It's effortless for him, like breathing or blinking or taking a shit when your bowels are working right and all you have to do is squat and let nature take its course. The assholery just comes right out. I don't exactly burst into sobs when she tells me he got jumped, but he's got me on a discount payment plan I can't complain about, and his coke is always beyond reproach, pure and unfucked-with and smelling of tropical rainforests.

User and provider. Demander and supplier. We depend on each other, Mick and I. Like the crocodile and the little bird whose name I can't remember that flosses bits of rotting flesh from the crocodile's teeth, what a documentary I saw once on *Planet Nature* calls a "symbiotic relationship."

An hour later I roll by her place on Valmont, windows down, stereo up so she can hear me coming down the street.

She's pissed, she knows I kept her waiting.

I make like I don't see her, cruise by like I'm on my way to pick up my dry cleaning. Not that I ever do dry cleaning. Wet cleaning isn't high up on my list of priorities either. Care less, sleep more.

I turn the corner, pull over.

I smoke the stub of a joint and call it breakfast.

I come back around ten minutes later and pass her again.

I stop at the end of the block and open the passenger door.

She doesn't move.

I honk.

She just stands there.

I lay on the horn.

I watch her in the rearview mirror staring at me.

People open their doors, stick their heads out of windows.

"Asshole!" someone yells. "Shut the fuck up!"

Finally she comes over.

"Need a ride?" I say.

"You're a child," she says. "It's sad."

She gets in, slams the door.

"I know you want to stick your tongue in my mouth," I say. "I might have dengue though—you don't know where I've been."

She lights a cigarette so she can blow smoke in my face.

"I know where you've been. I wouldn't go spreading the word. No glory in disgrace."

Maggie is Mick's girl, but she's got a thing for me, and I suppose I've got a thing for her. Thing is vague, I'm not sure what to call it. I know it has tough scales and nasty little teeth and hides under a rock. I kick it over now and then, and it hisses at me.

We don't hide it, though, flirt right in front of him. Which makes it look clean and innocent in Mick's eyes, like flirting with your friend's little sister. I'd have kissed a crowbar a long time ago if he thought for a moment we were for real. One way to know what the future has in store for you? Make a shitty decision with some long-term consequences.

Like Reggie Schexnayder, poor fuck. Pretty face, big smile. Squirrelling away change for dentures and reconstructive surgery. Didn't know where the lines are drawn. No use telling people, they'll just do what they want to do anyway. Everyone's got their own learning style.

It wouldn't be Mick. He'd have someone else do it, one of the bottom feeders who owes him. Jiffy or Carl or Angus or Julius— take your pick of degenerates. Lewis, if he wasn't pumping lead in some razor wire gym with tower guards. Someone I know so we can keep it in the family, cozy and close.

"Can we go?" she says. "Or do you just want to sit here and pick your nose?"

"Easy, I haven't turned on the meter yet."

I shift into gear and we go.

"So," I say.

"So what?"

"He'll live?"

She nods.

"But it was close?"

"Yeah," she says. "It was close."

I give her a look-over.

Sleeveless T-Rex top. Schoolgirl skirt with a jumbo brass safety pin holding the flaps together, but just barely. Chipped black nail polish. Fluorescent plastic ring. Eight tattoos, she says, but I've seen only five.

"You go to the hospital already? Last night?"

She shakes her head.

"I took a bunch of pills just before. The first nurse that saw me would've called the cops."

"Right. Better safe than sorry."

Something's on her mind. It's not Mick.

"What's up?"

"Nothing."

I feel the buffer, the drawn line. Back the fuck off.

"Any idea why? I mean Mick."

She shrugs.

"He's been selling some low-grade shit lately."

"Dissatisfied customer?"

"Yeah, well, you don't always get what you paid for."

He's also been moving bigger quantities, reaching out to suppliers in Dallas and Houston, crawling up the food chain.

"Maybe it's got nothing to do with that," I say. "Maybe it's just one of those things."

"What things?"

6

"This city."

"What are you talking about?"

"Everyone's packing. Everyone's got a gun or a knife. A goddamn mini bazooka in their trunk. Hand grenades bulging out of people's pockets."

"So?"

"Everyone's scared."

"Uh-huh. You too. I can tell."

"I'm not saying I'm not. I'm saying people do crazy shit when they're scared."

She shakes her head.

"The guy who stabbed Mick didn't do it because he was scared."

"I'm talking about a different kind of fear. Deeper."

"Too deep for me to understand. Right, got it. Thanks."

She turns away and looks out the window.

"That's not what I said," I say.

"It's what you meant."

We crawl with the morning traffic. Around us people are having their own shitty start of the day. On the bright side, it's encouraging to think we're moving in the same direction. Maybe it's all we can hope for. Maybe that's good enough.

Two years later and here we are. Some days it feels like nothing's changed. We watch the weather like we did before. We traffic in forecasts, dabble in prophecies. We dream of water. Tropic of Calamity. We know we're different from what we used to be, but we're not sure how. We've got a sickness in us, a slow-cooking madness that makes us not want to look in the mirror too closely. We came back to be in this together, and what we discovered is we don't remember how togetherness works anymore. We get to learn it again from scratch. We get to start over.

When Katrina hit, Maggie ran to her folks in Texas, got a job at a half tattoo parlor, half lefty bookshop up in Denton. Even had health insurance for a while. Two years later she got on a Greyhound in the middle of the night and rode it back to New Orleans. She didn't tell anyone she was coming back, didn't want to deal with the bullshit of goodbyes and well-intentioned people giving her very good reasons to stay put, make a new life for herself. She picks up stray shifts at Jack's, sells jewelry from a studio she shares with a Vietnamese woman on St. Mary.

We don't talk about it, but I know why she came back. Same reasons I did. The buzz of cicadas on a summer night. Spanish moss hanging from prehistoric live oaks like cobweb on Halloween. Thumb-sized roaches scuttling over the broken sidewalks. Endless porch sunsets. People calling passing strangers *honey* and *baby* and *how y'all doin'* like they're family. Mornings in the Quarter when the light is soft and cottony and the foggy air smells of the river, the hour when drunks come crawling out of bars and the sanitation crews with their trucks hose down the piss and the vomit and the tears off the streets, and it starts all over again, the naked hunger and the desperate love, your life feeling like a scratched record skipping and skipping, going nowhere, with nowhere to go.

We ride in silence.

She turns and looks at me.

"Can I ask you something?"

"Ask."

"Why didn't you stay in Pittsburgh?"

"Philly."

"Why didn't you?"

I shrug, light a cigarette.

"They got some shit up there called snow."

"That's not why."

"No. No, it's not."

"So?"

"Felt like a foreigner. Like I didn't belong, you know?"

She nods.

"And when they ask where you're from and you tell them the truth because it's too much work to make shit up, then it's all fake sympathy and shit about FEMA. And the fucking questions. Jesus. What was it like? How did you get away? Do you know someone who didn't? Did you lose your house? What about all your stuff? What's that feel like, losing everything? What are you going to do now? Until the compassion dries up and they start whispering behind your back, looking at you like you're a bum, living off of hand-outs like a parasite."

"I used to lie," she says. "I'd tell people I'm from somewhere else. Reno."

"Reno?"

"I don't even know what state it's in."

"Oregon, I think."

"You know, this thing with Mick . . ."

She stops. It's my cue. I'm supposed to nudge her. So we can pretend it's me who's getting it out of her, she's doing me a favor by talking about it.

I nudge her.

"What about it?" I say.

"Maybe it's a good thing," she says. "I mean it's not, it's horrible."

"But?"

"Maybe it's a sign. You believe in signs?"

"Sometimes. I've got selective faith."

"Telling me to get out, make a clean break. Maybe go back to Denton. Maybe Reno. But without a Category 5 breathing down my neck. You know what I mean?"

I nod.

"I've had time to think," she says. "I guess you too."

She wants me to tell her it's a great idea, we should all get out while we can, what we got was just a warning, a sneak preview. The locusts are swarming. The tide is rising again. Swim for the hills and don't look back. And if it doesn't work out in Denton or Reno or wherever, we'll pretend it's my fault, I talked her into it.

Not this time, I'm nipping this one in the bud.

"This isn't about me," I say.

She flicks the butt out the window.

"You're right. You've got your own shit to deal with."

"You mean I'm a selfish bastard who only thinks of himself."

"You're saying you're not?"

"It's not nice to be reminded for no good reason."

"You passed the hospital," she says.

She makes it sound like she knew I would, she didn't expect anything else from me.

It pisses me off. I'm not her goddamn errand boy. She can fuck off to Reno for all I care. I'll drive her there myself if she promises to stay put.

I slam on the breaks and skid a U-turn around a red light, get honked at and screamed at, clip the side view mirror off a parked car.

She's unimpressed.

"You're coming too," she says. "And slow the fuck down."

Visiting hours at Touro. Nauseating corridors. Hopeless whiteness. Stink of corrosive chemicals, cleansing fluids that rip open your sinuses and make your nose bleed.

No wonder you shiver, break out in sweat, get this feeling like maybe you should check yourself in, get yourself examined. Something tells you you've been on your way out for months now, for years. You've been dying inside a little bit every day and you had no clue, this is your last chance to get back on track, get tuned up. They're not making any promises, not considering the shape you're in, but late is better than never, maybe they can still save you, save some small part of you, good thing you stopped by when you did. Talk about lucky. Talk about happy accidents.

"You sure you don't want to go alone?" I say. "I can wait here, I don't mind."

"Don't be a pussy," she says. "He's not going to bite."

She asks for Mick and they give her a room number.

We pass an old couple sitting in the corner, staring at the floor, holding each other's withered papery hands.

We pass a man leaning his head on a window, fists clenched, one foot missing a shoe.

We pass a sprinting nurse with that look on her face nurses get when the beeping stops, the line goes flat and there's going to be a vacant bed soon.

I look away, take a deep breath and hold it until we pass her, a superstitious thing my mother used to do when she'd walk by some unlucky sign, a dead bird, a dead squirrel, so the bad luck wouldn't rub off on us. She was protecting the family.

"In here," Maggie says.

I exhale.

We walk in.

Mick grins at us from the bed.

"How nice," he says. "We've got ourselves a party now."

"Hey, baby," she says.

"What took you so long?"

She gives me a look.

"Traffic," I say. "Sorry."

"You bring me fruit and flowers?"

"You don't do fruit and flowers."

"How about cigarettes?"

I throw him my pack.

She fixes his pillow, kisses him.

First pillow, then kiss, in that order. I notice these things. I find meanings in them.

"How's the gut?" I say.

"Flesh wound," he says.

"Never really understood what that meant."

"Means I'm one lucky motherfucking fuck."

"Well I'm glad one of us is."

"Who was it?" she says. "Did you get a look at him?"

Apparently she didn't ask him this when they spoke on the phone. I notice that too.

"Black kid. Never saw him before in my life."

I look at her and she knows what I'm thinking. The deeper kind of scared. The kind that's pissed off and carries a blade.

"Cool as a meat locker," he says. "Walked up and shivved me and walked away. Barely even stopped. Like he was going somewhere and the idea suddenly popped in his head."

I get a flash, a Polaroid from a parallel universe. *Hard fluorescents. Shiny chrome and cold ceramic tiles. A guy in a white coat slides Mick out of a wall of corpse drawers.*

"That's crazy," she says. "That's insane, Mick."

Her phone rings. The mechanic.

She steps out, she has to take this.

Mick pats the bed, wants me to get comfy with him.

I get comfy.

He looks at me.

I wait.

"You know anything about this?" he says.

"Tell me you're shitting me," I say.

"Just asking."

"Fuck you, man."

"Just asking."

"Yeah, that's right, I forgot. I heard some guy talking he was going to stick a knife in you, but I thought, nah, I don't need to tell him, Mick can handle himself, he's a big boy."

"I think of you as my friend, Jimmy."

"I think of you too."

He pulls himself up. He gives me the icepick eyes.

"I think of you as someone who wouldn't bullshit me to my face," he says.

"Same here, sweetheart."

"You don't know anything about this?"

He's scared. He knows he came close on this one.

Maggie covering her mouth, me holding her, nodding to the guy in the coat, yep, that's him, Meatlocker Mick. Slide him back in, we've seen enough, we have to go, we have to keep moving.

"I don't know nothing, boss," I say. "Honest."

He smiles, pats me on the leg.

"I guess you have to trust someone," he says.
"What friends are for," I say.

O

I give her a ride to the mechanic.
She twirls her ring and doesn't say much.
I need a drink. I've been needing one all day.
"Want to stop at Molly's?" I say.
She lights a cigarette. Her hand trembles.
"What's the damage on the truck?"
She doesn't hear me.
"Maggie? What did the mechanic say?"
"I shouldn't have come back," she says.
To which I have nothing to say.
She looks at me, frowns.
"Jesus," she says. "Your nose."
I look in the mirror. A red trickle.
I look for something to wipe myself with.
"I don't have anything," she says. "I'm sorry."
I decide to ignore it. Fuck it, it's just blood.
"For fucksake," she says.
She goes to wipe it off with her hand.
I beat her to it, swipe my nose on my sleeve.
She sits back, looks out.
"It's the chemicals," I say. "From the hospital."
She's silent.
"The clutch is fried," she says. "It's a total waste."

Big Tom cracks open a beer, drains it, crushes the can.

Starter beer, he says, you don't linger over that one.

He starts sharpening a fillet knife.

"How's the patient?" he says.

We're in the kitchen at Jack's doing prep for the night. Or you could say we're handling sharp objects stoned, it's a question of perspective.

"He'll pull through," I say. "Flesh wound."

"He called me. He tell you that? Wanted to know if I knew anything. Like if I heard someone was out to get him."

"What did you say?"

"Told him to go fuck himself, paranoid bastard."

"How'd he take that?"

"He said some weird shit about how we're friends and how he trusts me. I don't know what kind of drugs they got him on. It gives me the creeps."

"He's scared."

"Yeah, well, he should be. He had it coming, if you ask me. Selling out in the alley, in the parking lot. Middle of the goddamn shift. He got greedy, man, that's what happened. You get greedy, you get stupid. You get stupid, you get reckless. Cause and effect. Then you wonder why shit happens."

He'd never say it to Mick's face and he knows I'm not going to repeat it to him. Work in kitchens long enough and you adopt an ethical code. Never rat. Never repeat what's told to you in confidence.

"You buy from him too," I say.

"Not anymore. I'm done with him and his shit."

Tom's not exactly a model citizen and it pisses me off when he climbs the pulpit. Busted twice for possession, restraining order courtesy of the ex, more DUIs than I got parking tickets. Says he has a drinking problem. Says his problem is he can't drink enough. Funny the first time.

There's a story Tom likes to tell. He was drinking and walking in the Quarter one afternoon. He'd just finished his tall boy and he's holding this brown paper sack that he's about to throw away. He sees a cop and a thought occurs to him. He puffs up the bag, walks over to the cop, stands behind him, and blows it up in his ear. The cop jumps. Tom laughs in his face. An epic chase ensues. Down Dauphine and across Elysian Fields, into the Marigny all the way down to St. Rock. The cop catches him in front of Schiro's Café, tackles him to the ground. Tom smells booze on the guy's face and realizes the cop is drunk. New Orleans' Finest, vigilant and everready. Tom tries to push him off. But the cop's had enough, he's tired, he's not doing this anymore. He swings and lands a wallop of a punch in Tom's face, breaks his nose with an audible crack, like someone snapping a twig. So here's what Tom does. He starts to laugh. He hugs the cop and tells him that's never happened to him before, he's a big guy, no one ever broke his nose with one goddamn punch. This is a special occasion, he tells him, it calls for a celebration. And now this is the really good part. A cop walks into a bar with a guy twice his size and a bloody face and they sit and do back-to-back shots. They get so rowdy by the end of the night, the bartender has to ask them to leave. Possibly it's all bullshit. The time he held up a liquor store with a water pistol. The time he broke a prostitute out of jail in Singapore and proposed to her, only to find out she had a husband and five kids. The time he licked pussy for three hours straight. His tongue cramped up so bad he had to drive to the ER to get a shot of muscle relaxer. Then he went back for more. Fucked if I know how much of it is true. Fucked if I care.

Now Andy, Tom's little brother, he's for real. A couple of tours in Iraq, working at Virgil's Kitchen across the street from Jack's. You don't need ten fingers to wash dishes. You can go autopilot, zone out all night and no one gives a shit as long as the plates are clean and the pots are stacked right.

I come by Tom's place now and then. He's always got fresh weed and likes to put a little cash down on a fight, and Andy's sitting in the same spot on the couch, staring at the TV. I've seen him watching it when it isn't even on. He doesn't seem to notice. Dead screen for dead eyes.

Never talks about it, pretends like nothing happened over there. Or doesn't want to remember. And why the fuck would he? It's not like he came back from Candyland with pockets full of treasure and a head full of happy thoughts, like reporters want to hear his side of the story, put him on a glossy cover, like he's got book deals and movie deals and five-star generals come knocking on his door to pin medals on his chest. Yesterday's hero, old news. Ghosts like that are a dime a dozen.

He smiles when I come over, mumbles a spineless hello. I can't always say for sure he knows it's me, though. Still, I guess he can at least tell the friendlies from the enemy combatants, the goodies from the baddies.

Handy Andy. He went around the house fixing things when he was a kid. Busted kitchen drawers, broken radios, making things whole again, giving them a second life, a second chance. Wanted to be a carpenter, says Tom. Carpenter. What kind of kid wants to be a carpenter, for fucksake?

Not anymore, though. He's cured of that now.

Andy. Ghostboy.

He never came back to us.

Somewhere out there is an endless burning desert, and he's in it all alone. It's dead quiet and he's holding his hand up, shielding his eyes from the sun.

He licks his parched lips.

He looks up, squinting.

Dark shapes circle above him in the cloudless sky.

Great shadows with black wings.

4

Next night I have off. Maggie's not answering her phone so I call Darryl. Otherwise it's just me and some so-so weed and reruns of *M*A*S*H*.

"Meet you at Rock 'n' Bowl," says Darryl.

"You're going to stand me up again," I say.

"Did I tell you I'm opening a barber shop?"

"No, you cocksucker."

He laughs.

"One hour," he says. "I'm buying."

Two hours later I'm on beer five, Darryl's still MIA, and I'm seriously considering stealing Tom Cruise's bowling shoes. Story is he was making the vampire film and came in from the shoot one night to bowl. Probably sucked at it, should've hired a double to roll for him, but they just couldn't wait to get the shoes off his feet and nail them to the wall above the stairs. No one's touched them since, they're sacred, Tom fucking Cruise's feet were in them.

I'm thinking of some other holy relics I'd like to get my hands on, start a collection, get me some purpose in life.

Donald Trump's hairpiece.

Larry King's suspenders.

Leonard Nimoy's Vulcan ears.

Jon Voigt's hat from *Midnight Cowboy*.

Madonna's cone-shaped bra from *Like a Virgin*.

Madonna's thong.

Madonna's used tampon.

We're all suckers that way. The magic's elsewhere, you're not special, your shit stinks, your blood's as negative as the next guy's. No one wants to freeze your DNA for the benefit of future generations. Your funeral won't be broadcast to millions of weepy worshippers across the globe.

"Hey, Jimmy!"

I turn and Tom swings a bowling ball at my face.

I feel the wind as it just misses my nose.

He thinks it's funny as fuck.

"Try that again and I'll bite your ear off," I say.

I'm looking at his ear, fat and meaty. I'm not kidding.

"Come knock down some pins with me and Andy," he says.

"Andy's here?"

Andy doesn't go out much. Tom does the shopping, cooking, cleaning. He scrubs Andy's soiled underwear before taking it to the Laundromat. A full-grown man who sleeps with the bedroom door open and the hallway light on. A boy with night frights, with monsters under his bed.

Shitty diapers. No one needs to see that sort of thing. It's undignified.

Because I want to see how someone can bowl with only three fingers, I walk over with Tom and we stand behind Andy. A crowd has gathered to watch him, he's got a fan club going.

"You seen Darryl around?" I say.

"Shh," he says. "Watch this."

But nothing's happening. Andy's frozen. He holds the ball up to his nose, stares at the pins, doesn't move, doesn't even seem to be breathing.

I look at Tom.

He winks to say *wait for it, wait for it.*

But Andy is off in his desert. Vultures are circling and calling his name, mirages are warping in the distance, melting like broken promises.

Then he cracks his neck.

He tackles the lane, swings, releases.

The ball slams down and speeds, curves way right, skims the gutter, suddenly swerves back as if rebuffed by some invisible force and cleans the pins from the side.

It's Ballistics 101. It's an execution.

"Never misses," says Tom. "Couldn't miss if he wanted to. That right there's military training. Say what you want about the war, but we're getting some fine bowlers courtesy of the U.S. government."

"Except when they come back with no arms," I say. "I guess they can always play Hacky Sack or hopscotch. Presuming they still have legs."

Tom grunts. I'm missing the point.

Andy comes over, beaming. He has that glint in his eye he can still sometimes get.

"We win," he says.

"We do that, bro," Tom says. "We like winning."

He throws an arm around his neck, kisses him on the cheek.

"You get the money?"

Andy nods.

"Attaboy."

A pretty girl walks by, mouthing the teeny pop song playing on the jukebox, bouncy dress jumping to her skip-step.

"Sweet mother of Jesus Christ," says Tom.

He elbows Andy.

"How long has it been? Your pecker must be going stir-crazy. What do you say? Time to shoot the gun? I think so. I think tonight's the night."

Andy looks at me. He wants me to help.

I shrug.

Maggie said it, I've got my own shit to deal with.

"All right," says Tom.

He turns Andy around to face the bar.

"Which one, that's the question. How's that little blonde over there on the left? Fancy fucking her up the ass?"

That's it, I'm out. I'm done with Big Brother the pimp and Ghostboy the shell-shocked bowling genius. I'm giving Darryl ten more minutes and then he can go fuck himself with a broomstick.

I get a beer and walk over to watch the Zydeco band getting ready to play. It's three old white men and a black girl. They joke and laugh. She calls one of them "Papa," but he's not her father, he's just an old man and she's a young girl.

She touches his shoulder.

He looks up and smiles.

I squeeze the beer bottle, fight off something suddenly welling up inside me.

Then I want to let it out. But it's gone, it's passed. I can't bring it back.

They start to play. She sings, uses a spoon to strum the washboard strapped to her chest.

She looks at me.

I raise my beer.

She smiles and looks away.

I don't want to know her name, I don't want to talk to her. I want to leave it like this. We'll never fall in love. We'll never break each other's hearts with lies and unkind words.

Something's up at the bar.

Chairs knocked over, glass shattering, girl screaming.

Andy on top of a guy in a frat shirt, punching his face.

I get what happened, no need for subtitles on this. She's got a boyfriend, he wasn't amused, words were exchanged, someone shoved someone and Andy's off fighting the insurgents, giving his all for freedom and democracy and the American way of life.

Except it's not like that, they say. It's the man next to you that you're fighting for, your brother in arms. They teach you camaraderie, not political philosophy.

Tom watches, grins. He lights a cigarette.

The bouncer grabs Andy, gets an elbow in the groin.

I turn and walk.

I give Tom Cruise's shoes a parting glance.

Too high. They knew what they were doing nailing them way the fuck up there.

Something wet on my face. Fleshy and sandpapery.
Whining. Bad breath. More whining.

Pike.

"Okay, okay," I say. "I'm getting up."

He looks at me. He doesn't believe me.

"I don't blame you," I say.

Love your four-legged friend? Feed it, walk it. Rub its head now and then and it'll think you're God. Treat it like shit it and it'll still think you're God.

"I'm standing," I say. "See? Both feet. Okay?"

He smiles.

We split an omelet and go for a walk.

He stops often, looks back, gives me time to catch up. He knows mornings aren't easy for me.

We turn on Esplanade, over Rampart, down Dauphine into the morning graveyard of the Quarter.

We stop in Jackson Square by the cathedral.

I tie Pike to a lamppost and walk in to cool off.

I sit in a pew in the back.

I inhale the churchy smell of burning wax.

When I was ten, a girl I had a crush on in school told me this is how God smells. I don't know how she knew, but it left an impression. I think of heaven as this big quiet place where they never open the windows and only whispering is allowed.

Just a few stragglers about. It's the intermission between services, the slow hour.

What they need, I'm thinking, is a happy hour instead, something to draw in the tourists looking to escape the heat. Cold beers and couples discounts in the confessional. Free candles. Church swag in goodie bags.

But the Church is old and crusty and slow to change. What they need is a more entrepreneurial Pope to pass the Happy Hour Edict, some guy with a business degree from Harvard and a *Times* bestseller on corporate efficiency. It should be a cinch under the right management. Clerics were the first bankers, it's not like they lack the experience.

I step out into the sun with big ideas about ecclesiastical reform.

Pike has taken the opportunity to relieve himself. He's half-lying in his piss, head resting on his paws, looking fat and tired.

"Sorry, boy. I should've left you some water. But I can see you made your own."

He raises his eyes, blinks sadly.

"Sorry," I say. "Bad joke."

A fortune-teller with gypsy-style jangles hanging from her overcomplicated dress is giving me the evil eye. She means the dog's disgraceful conduct, and she means my disgraceful conduct apropos the dog's urination. Especially on holy ground. It's bad form.

She means more than that, too. People like me are part of a bigger problem. People who would take a shit anywhere, who have no regard for public property and communal well being and a sense of shared destiny. The degenerates who didn't get washed away in the flood. Detritus.

I consider crossing her palm with silver so she can tell me what I have to look forward to. Except it's always the long perspective you get, the view from twenty thousand feet.

I've experienced some hardships lately?

You could say that, yes.

I've been in love and it didn't work out?

Wow, bull's-eye.

I find it hard to trust people?

Me again.

But good news. See this line, one that looks like a river?

Yes, I see it.

See how it crosses The Valley of Horseshit and flows into The Fields of Future Joy?

Which means?

My luck's about to change. But it's up to me. I need to keep my eyes open, let opportunity in when she comes knocking.

Tuesday nights I get naked in front of room full of people. I stand on a platform and they watch me in silence for an hour.

Darryl turned me on to it. Easy money, he said. You're just a slab of meat up there, just something for them to copy down on paper. They're not looking at you, he said, they're looking at lines and shadows, angles and proportions.

But they look. I feel them looking. You can't stare at a naked person that long and not wonder. At some point the thought's just there. Would I put it in him? Would I let him put it in me?

Lines and shadows and hard-ons.

Normally I get to sit or stand, do whatever I like as long as I can hold it for ten, twenty minutes. Tonight the drawing instructor wants me to crouch and make like I'm going to sprint. Tension in the muscles is what they're looking for, the torque of the tensed-up body, the moment before it springs into action.

Legs spread apart, balls hanging unencumbered, palms pressed down, my ass up in the air. Anything for art.

I listen to the scuffing of charcoal on paper and I think of reasons to run.

Dead-end restaurant job. Tom's bullshit. Mick's bullshit. Jack's bullshit. Jack's racist jokes that everyone's supposed to laugh at.

The hot grease you inhale gets inside your lungs, gets down into your bones. It lubricates you so you can work faster, work harder. It rots you out from the inside.

Burns and cuts up and down my arms like a failed suicide.

Coke habit creeping up. Can't call it "recreational" if you're on a payment plan.

Need to make a clean break. Start exercising, subscribe to a popular science magazine, expand my horizons.

Now and then this pain under the ribs. Don't want to know what that's about.

Pike's happy at least. Or doesn't know better, poor fuck.

Losing hair, forgetting things.

What was I going to be when I grew up? Deep-sea diver? Firefighter? Fuck-up?

Community college dropout. Apple of my mother's eye, pride of my father's loins. That's what sons are for. Inheritors of the line, carriers of the family name.

A Shakespeare scholar. I couldn't make myself go to his funeral. I wrote a letter to my mother that I didn't send. We don't talk.

They buried him with The Collected Works of The Bard. All of Shakespeare sitting on his chest. My mother's idea. So he has something familiar to grab on to when he wakes up. Othello and Lear and Macbeth and Roger Bogdan Petrovich. Like a party he walked in on and was surprised to see he knew everyone there.

O

Class over.

This time it doesn't feel like easy money, it feels like I worked for it. Pins and needles in my legs, my back telling me it doesn't like this very much, I'll find out tomorrow what a shitty idea this was.

I'm putting my clothes on behind the screen and this girl I've seen before is taking her time packing up her art things, dropping pencils, faking clumsiness, working up the courage.

I come out and she shoves a note into my hand, can't look me in the eye, dashes off.

I open it.

ZOË 9751296

Lines and shadows. Running in place.

7

Maggie gets a hold of me at Jack's. There's a party later in the Quarter, she says, a welcome-back thing for Mick. Also it's the birthday of the guy hosting, Daniel or Damien or someone, a trust fund kid with a taste for Mick's blow.

"How's he doing?" I say.

"They've got him doped up. Plenty enough to share."

She means it as an enticement, but she knows I'm not big on downers, head-foggers, cotton-brainers. I'll drop one now and then, sure, everyone needs to park the car once in a while. It's nothing like what I get from coke, though. The rocket rush, the quick trip to the moon. That feeling like I'm coming up for air, breaking the surface, inhaling pure light. Clarity, sharp and focused like the crack of a whip.

It's a slow night, Jack lets me off early. I hop a freight train down the levee and into the Quarter, detour into Molly's for a pint, decide to try Darryl.

"This is Darryl," he says.

"You stood me up, asshole," I say.

"Tell it like it is," says the recording.

I leave the address. I know he's not going to show.

I dig up Zoë's number.

"Zoë?"

Her voice is whispery.

"Yeah?"

She's been waiting, hoping I'd call, maybe starting to hope I don't, thinking maybe she made a mistake, I could be a total asshole, I could be a psychopath and now I have her number.

"Jim. From art class. What are you doing tonight?"

Tonight?

Does she want to come to a party?

What kind of party?

The good kind.

Sure. Okay. Yes. Where?

I tell her.

Does she need to bring anything?

That drawing she did of me today. I want to see it.

She laughs.

Not on a first date, she says.

O

I'm looking at Daniel's or Damien's house, and I'm calling Maggie a lying tramp.

There's a fluffy pink bunny on the porch, the animal head hanging limp upside-down behind the man head, like the bunny tried to swallow him whole but it was too much for him.

Bunny sees me climbing the porch steps, moves to block the entrance. He's not cuddly.

"You invited?"

This part I more or less expected. Passwords and secret hand-shakes, private clubs and private parties, circles within circles. There are parts of the Quarter you'll never see if you're not on the inside, drawbridges that won't come down unless you know people. Or people who know people.

Bunny the Bouncer. This isn't exactly the innermost circle but it's far enough from the fringe to require prior intimacy.

"I'm here with Maggie."

"Don't know a Maggie. You a friend of Daniel's?"

"I'm a friend of Mick's."

"Yeah, Mick's here," says Bunny.

Mick the candy man, life of the party. If I'm lucky he's up in the clouds, handing our freebies, feeling good about not having a mortuary tag on his toe. Meatlocker Mick, resurrected.

Bunny lets me pass.

"Nice costume," I say. "Very authentic."

A gorilla comes out as I walk in. By the way it's pawing Bunny, I figure it's a female of the species. I can't be sure, though, apes are too close to us to make safe predications.

Inside it's more animals, harlequins in checkered spandex, randy Pinocchios with cock-shaped noses, the usual stock of angels and devils, nurses in black fishnets and three-inch skirts dying to take your pulse, Catholic school girls begging to be disciplined, geriatric vampires rubbing up against nubile Snow Whites, Little Red Riding Hoods on the prowl for Big Bad wolves. Mardi Gras out of season, Halloween out of focus.

I pour myself a drink and walk around. High ceilings with teardrop chandeliers. Mirrors tall and wide enough to reflect all your multiple personalities. Rooms with Louis-Somethingth furniture and old-time portraits of white people in powdered wigs. A life-sized sculpture of a nude couple making out, their limbs twisted around each other like ferocious snakes. A tiny Japanese tree on top of a marble pedestal. Orchids flowering with joy. They know how good they have it.

Lines and shadows everywhere. Animals in twos and threes wait in front of closed doors for their turn inside. You're out of luck if you need to take a piss. That is unless you don't mind a little company. Me, I like to be alone when nature calls. It's the least I can do for what's left of my dignity.

"Take your shirt off."

I turn.

A bumpkin in overalls. Dirty feet, messy face, chewing on a toothpick. No shirt, no bra. Just like the real thing.

"Thanks for telling me it's a costume party," I say.

"I thought you knew," Maggie says.

"Right. Because you told me."

"Take off your shirt."

"Why?"

"Just do it, Jim."

I do it.

She sticks a marker in her mouth and bites off the cap.

"Hold still," she says.

She writes on my chest.

I look down. It says I'm

FREE MEAT

"There. You've got a costume."

"My meat's not free," I say.

"Relax, Jimmy."

"I am relaxed."

"No, you're not. You're tense. Why are you so clenched? Why can't you just . . ."

"Just what?"

"Nothing. Forget it. Christ, you're fucking difficult, did you know that?"

Eyes glittering like black diamonds. Ecstasy is my guess, sandwiched between rails of coke.

"Mick here?"

But she's not listening, she's got her sights fixed on the nearest door, looks like a walk-in closet. Three fairy-taleish creatures are waiting for their turn to go in.

A mummy steps out trailing bandages, followed by a raggedy Southern debutante or beauty pageant contestant, it's difficult to tell from what's left.

The fairy-tale creatures go in and shut the door.

Maggie gives me a look.

I raise a brow.

She sighs, slaps me on the ass.

"Next time, meat man."

She walks off.

I reach to grab her, miss.

Next time.

I raise my eyes, see Alex from *A Clockwork Orange*. Mick. He's been watching us.

I walk over to say hello.

"Patched up and good as new?" I say.

He smiles.

"Top of the world."

"Excellent place to be."

"But it's a long way down," he says.

Shielding his side with his elbow, protecting the wound. Still scared. But he's safe here, he's among friends. Or at least among paying customers, which is even better. He feels needed. He feels loved.

"You heard Jack fired me?" he says.

I nod.

"What the fuck," he says. "Right?"

"Blows."

Jack called him to tell him he's had enough of his shit and Tom brought Andy in to try out for the line cook job. Ghostboy did his best. Drifting around the kitchen like a sleepwalker, dropping plates, scorching thirty-dollar French-cut lamb chops. I heard Jack tell Tom Andy's not going to work out, the place has a reputation to maintain, Jack had to strap on an apron himself and pitch in when the dinner rush came, he can't be doing that.

But he pulled Tom aside to tell him quietly, no need to embarrass the boy. I saw him give Andy a hundred at the end of the night, pat his back. It was generous, sure, but it was also redemption money, laundering a dirty conscience. Jack used to have a bumper sticker that said

FREEDOM
GET WITH IT
OR GET OUT!

He tried to strip it off when coffins draped with American flags started flying, but the glue was too strong. Now it says

R ED M
GET W TH
G OUT!

"Fuck him," says Mick. "I got a new job."

"Doing the disaster tour again?"

He shakes his head.

"That's all dead. Glutted market. I work in a kite shop. Want to buy a kite?"

"I can't ever get those things off the ground."

But he's not trying to sell me a kite. He wants to sell me something else.

"Come with me, Jimbo," he says. "There's someone I want you to meet."

I follow Mick, then lose him in a crowd in the next room.

I spot Maggie talking to Jiffy. He came as a werewolf, or maybe it's just mangy dog trying to stand on its hind legs.

I spot Darryl. The fucker actually showed up.

But when I get close I see it's not him.

We've all got them, doubles, spooky look-alikes. Don't run into yours or you're both fucked, you'll cancel each other out.

I stop to look at a display case with Civil War era swords, pistols, medals. Speckled with blood or rust, I can't tell.

I look into a room where a silent crowd is watching someone doing something to someone on the floor.

I elbow my way through the zoo in the kitchen and stumble out the back door into big walled-in yard where a breeze from heaven hits my face and cools me off, the letters on my chest running like cheap mascara.

Mick's waiting.

"Go talk to that guy," he says.

A Christmas elf sitting at a table under an oak tree. Legs crossed, head tilted back, smoking a cigar. Santa's Little Helper on his night off.

"Him?"

Mick takes my empty glass.

"Be right back," he says.

I walk over to the elf.

Late thirties, early forties. Rhett Butler moustache, dark eyes, strong jawbone. The sort you can't help but like because he reminds you of someone famous.

The elf outfit looks expensive and tailored, like it might actually be the real thing and not a costume at all. He looks weirdly dapper in it.

He looks at my chest, reads it, grins.

I don't blame him.

"Jim, right?"

"That's right."

A soap actor, maybe, or the guy on late-night infomercials whose face gets seared in your brain because that's the time of day when you're most vulnerable to suggestion. I've heard it's a scientific fact, your buffer is down and you're just sponging it in. The sharpest knife in the whole world, the best toilet scrubber on the market, the last screwdriver you'll ever buy.

"Nice to meet you," he says.

No, he'd be pushing something you really want, something you could actually use.

We shake, I sit.

His name is Ron, he says. Ron Dan is his full name, first and last, in that order. Lots of people get it wrong, he says, it's a little confusing.

"Lots of confused people out there," I say. "It can't be all your fault."

He's a natural-born grinner. He inspires confidence.

"Shall we make small talk first or do we want to get right to it?" he says.

"I'll take what's behind Door Number Two."

"Mick speaks highly of you. He says you're a good guy. He says you're reliable."

Here's the pitch. I run through a few plays in my head but wait to see what he'll throw at me before I swing.

"I'll be straightforward with you," he says. "Because it's a straightforward kind of job."

Works for me, I say.

Did Mick say anything to me?

He didn't.

Just as well. Do I like music? Blues, jazz?

Sure, what's not to like.

He's a writer, he says. He's writing a book on Mongoose.

"You might know him if you're a jazz aficionado," he says.

I shrug.

"No? Walter 'Mongoose' Johns?"

"Sorry."

"A living legend. Played with Ollie Brixton, Longhorn Day and Merle Wolfe, Ellis Horton in the days of The Horton Five."

"Never heard of him."

"No wonder, actually. He never made a recording, avoided the spotlight, quit playing when he was just entering his prime. By all accounts he was an incredible musician, one of those greats who somehow slip through the cracks of history."

"It happens," I say.

He nods, blows on his cigar cherry.

"What I'm doing is sort of like archeology. I want to dig him up, dust him off. I want people to know who he was. Who he still is. I've done a lot of research and I'm still digging. A biographer ought to know as much as possible about his subject. It's an obligation I mean to uphold. But what I've got right now is really just odds and ends, scraps and gossip."

"He's still alive?"

"And sharp as ever."

"So why not just ask him?"

"I've tried. He won't talk to me."

"Because?"

"He says those days are behind him. Friends, family, no one will talk to me. Apparently I've been blacklisted."

"What about all those guys he used to play with?"

"Dead. Or they can't recall more than an anecdote or two."

"Okay, so?"

"So. I've got a contract for a book I can't write. I mean I can't write it the way it should be written."

"Which is?"

"Honestly. Truthfully."

"And you need someone to what? Shake it out of him? Look, I don't know what Mick's been telling you about me, but—"

"All I said is you're the man for the job," says Mick.

He sits, hands me a drink.

"Just talk to him," says Ron. "Get him to open up."

"You mean be an informant."

"More like a fact checker," says Ron.

"Confidence man," says Mick. "In a manner of speaking."

"Here's the bottom line," says Ron. "My deadline is coming up, and I've got more unconfirmed rumors than I know what to do with. I need a change of strategy, I need to find another way in. And I have a feeling this just might work. At this point I've got nothing to lose, anyway. What do you say?"

"Come on, you're a writer," says Mick. "This is right up your alley."

"You write?" says Ron.

I shake my head.

I once showed Maggie a short story I wrote. She let Mick read it without asking me. Somehow the fact that he liked it made the betrayal feel even worse.

"You'll be sort of like a filter," Mick says. "Separate the wheat from the chaff."

"Why would he talk to me? He doesn't know me."

"That's exactly right," says Ron. "He doesn't know you, you don't know him. You're just two people talking. I'll help you, I don't expect you to jump into it blind."

"You've got a baby face," says Mick. "You've got a face people trust. Like me, I trust you. So does Ron. Right?"

Ron smiles.

A friend of Mick's is a friend of Mick's.

The pay's a thousand a week, says Ron. Four, maybe five weeks, he can't go longer than that.

"Easy money," says Mick.

"Fair pay," says Ron.

The publisher was generous with the advance, he says, a big art-grant-funded house on the lookout for New Orleans stories, tales of hardship and woe, the resilience of the human spirit, extraordinary lives lived by ordinary people. And they think it will sell. New Orleans is hot right now, but who knows for how long, calamities have a shelf life. He's not doing it for the paycheck, though, he's not trying to jump on the disaster wagon. He's doing it because it's the right thing to do, tell a story that needs to be told.

"Fucking bestseller," says Mick.

"A decent book," says Ron. "I'd be happy with that."

Ron the decent do-right Christmas elf. Makes me want to believe in Santa and the Tooth Fairy all over again.

"I already have a job," I say.

"A shit job," says Mick. "You can always go back. Jack will take you, he's done it before."

Like when I quit two years ago to paint houses with Darryl for the summer. Jack wasn't thrilled but he took me back, he knows I work my ass off every night.

I look at Mick.

"What about you?" I say. "You know about wheat and chaff."

"Yeah, but would you talk to me? Look at this mug."

He shows me a profile. He's got a point.

"Look, Jimbo. When that fucker stabbed me, who came to see if I'm still kicking? You. I owe you."

"Think about it," says Ron. "I can wait a couple of days, but then I'm going to have to look elsewhere. I'm running out of time."

He takes out his wallet, hands me a card.

RON K. DAN
SOUND OF MUZIK
504.126.1178
ron.dan@freemail.com

"You got a typo here," I say.

A local music e-zine, he says. He writes for them occasionally, it keeps him in shape.

"And it helps pays for groceries," he says. "Meat's not free. Regardless of what the advertisements around here say." He grins. Fucker couldn't resist after all.

Mick uncaps a ballpoint pen, takes a snort, offers.

Ron says not him, he's calling it a night.

Mick walks him out.

Maggie brings me a beer, pinches my cheek, wanders off.

I take a bump from Mick's pen and mull it over.

A grand a week versus two-fifty at Jack's. And he'll take me back, Mick's got a point, I've got job security, something to consider the next time I want to make a list of reasons to run.

O

Quarter past three.

Inside the zoo's thinned out, several species are extinct.

On my way out I spot Zoë 9751296 with Werewolf Jiff.

How did she get past Bunny? Did he leave his post? Does she also know people? No, I figure it's just animal nature. She came as free meat but doesn't know it.

Jiff. Lives in the only house I know in New Orleans that has a basement. Cooks meth in it.

He's watching her, licking his chops like werewolves do, and she's chirping away, waving her arms, spilling her drink. She's a clueless baby gazelle and I know what's coming, I've seen this nature documentary before. It's not going to be pretty.

I stand there and watch them, and I get this feeling like I'm standing at a crossing, a forking of paths. Parallel worlds touching, bumping into each other in the dark and endless ether and parting ways never to meet again. I could end up in either one. I just have to jump. I just have to move.

Valley of Horseshit. Fields of Future Joy.

You can extend that line on your palm with an X-Acto knife.

You can use your goddamn fingernail if you really need to.

Zoë turns and scans the room.

She sees me. She waves.

She turns back and says something to Jiffy.

He laughs, nods, sticks a cigarette in his mouth.

She lights it for him.

They keep talking.

I turn and walk.

I pass by the swords and pistols and think about the times men called each other out on duels. I think about the men who got themselves killed for nothing. *Honor*, they called it.

Who knows their names anymore?

Not me.

I cook a cauldron of coffee.

I take a cold shower and screw my head back on.

I do ten push-ups just to see what happens.

Panting and heaving is what happens, blood pounding in my ears, blurred vision. Best not to push my luck.

I take a heroic shit. The pain in my side wakes up, then subsides. Just pent up feelings, it turns out. Maybe Maggie's right, I'm wound too tight, I need to learn to unclench.

I crank up the desktop, look up Ron Dan. I skim articles he's written about the music scene in San Francisco, Detroit, New Orleans. He likes to use big words like *chiaroscuro* and *Weltanschauung*.

Sound of Muzik. Ron's an *editor-at-large*. It sounds like something without a horizon. There's a picture of him smiling his effortless smile, looking fresh and dapper, lucky and easy.

I click on his resume. Awards for music journalism, hosted a radio show in D.C., did a stint at *Rolling Stone*. Accolades and accomplishments.

He's written two books. A biography of Dorian Zak, lead singer for a band called Lawless Mindy, and a more recent one about a New Orleans rapper by the name of N-Zime.

I download some Lawless Mindy tracks. "My Latrine" and "mistercocainebonehard" from *Sick of You, Sick of Me.* "Empathy Curfew" and "Fangassss" from *King of Zero.* If you've got nothing to say, you might as well say it loud.

N-Zime. Bitches and hoes and Ninth-Ward drive-bys. The daily news, in other words. I'll take Mindy and a bag of popcorn.

I do a search on "Walter Johns."

"Mongoose."

"Walter Mongoose."

"Mongoose Johns."

I find close to nothing.

A living legend, Ron called him. Sure, I believe it. This city is overflowing with living legends, we've got a surplus, we should export them. The deranged soapbox preacher on Canal Street with the cracked megaphone and rainbow umbrella hat is a living legend. So is the silver-painted mime who poses for dimes on a milk carton in Jackson Square and who they say was an opera singer in a former life. And the burnt-out streetcar driver screaming at cars on St. Charles to get out of his fucking way or he'll ram them is a legend. He's not kidding, I've seen him do it. Dive bars and jailhouses and state nursing homes packed with living legends, all of them special and unique, all of them forgotten by the world in their own special way.

Fact checker. Informant. Snoop. Spy.

Four grand. Five, if I can stretch it.

I could go places with that kind of money. I could start over. I could even go to Reno if I had a reason to.

I dial Ron, get a machine.

"Ron, Jim. Call me when you get this."

I call the restaurant to tell Jack something's come up, I need to take some time off.

He growls.

"What do you mean *something*?"

44

He's knocked back a few and it's gone down the wrong way.

"I saw a doctor," I say. "He says I need to ease up."

"Ease up?"

"He says I've been pushing myself too hard."

"What you need is to lay off the blow," he says. "That's what you need."

"It's just for a while."

"What's a while?"

"Month, maybe."

"Fuck off," he says.

"Listen, Jack—"

"No, really, fuck off for this. You know what I like even less than sending my wife an alimony check every fucking month? Less than the ass surgery I'm going to get? For the cancer growing on my ass? Your fucking lack of respect. For me, for my business, for my livelihood. You don't give a shit, Jimmy. We're done."

I might as well do what I told him I did. I call Tom, ask him for the name of his doctor.

"What do you want a doctor for?"

"Oil change."

"Tune-up? I have just the guy for you."

I call, ask to make an appointment with Dr. Kusznierewicz.

I'm in luck, says the nurse, someone just canceled, the doctor can see me in four weeks.

"I'm a lucky guy," I say.

"Good for you, sweetie," she says.

Her name is Lori. She sounds like someone's grandmother, the kind that bakes cookies for the patients.

I ask her if there's a discount for lucky guys with no health insurance.

There isn't, she says, but maybe the symptoms will go away. It happens all the time, seventy-three percent of the cases they see turn out to be psychosomatic.

"Seventy-three? That's an actual statistic?"

"Just think of something nice for the rest of the day. Your fondest childhood memory, for instance."

"I don't have a fondest childhood memory."

I open a beer. I'm making progress, doing something about my health, thinking about the future. I should be rewarded.

I cut a tight line of blow but then change my mind, light a joint instead, stretch out on the couch and reward myself with a nice long wank.

I drift off content, almost happy.

O

"Wake up," she says.

I open my eyes.

A girl. She's giving me this sad-disgusted look, like I'm a drunk passed out on the sidewalk.

I must have left the door open. Or she came in through the window. I've done it a couple of times when I lost my keys.

I check my fly, make sure nothing's hanging out. Not that it should matter, a man's home is his castle.

"Who the fuck are you?"

Slim and pale. Blue-eyed. Strawberry blonde hair cropped short. Dark lipstick and freckles. T-shirt, jeans, army boots. Laptop case slung over her shoulder. Hand on her hip. Sucking a lollipop.

She yanks it out. It's pink.

"Willi," she says.

"Okay. What the fuck are you doing here, Willi?"

Pike nuzzles her hand, licks it.

I throw a shoe at him, miss.

"I'm Ron's niece. You called him, remember? I have your instructions."

She pulls an envelope from the laptop case. It says

JIM

She holds it out. I'm supposed to go get it.

I don't.

She shrugs, drops it on the table.

She twitches her nose, makes a sour face.

"What are you doing?" I say.

"It smells like rat in here."

"What does rat smell like exactly?"

"Like this."

The lollipop hops back in where it's wet and warm and cozy.

"I never said I'd take it," I say. "The job."

"No?"

"Not to my recollection."

She puts on a sad-puzzled look.

Then she brightens up.

"Wait, I get it! This is the part where you say you're not interested unless we renegotiate the pay. Something like that? You also want health insurance and a parking permit."

"It would be nice, actually."

"A thousand a week," she says. "Take it or leave it."

I pull myself up.

She stares back.

"Ron's niece?"

"We've established that already," she says. "Are we just going to keep doing this? Is this something you do, repeating what you already know?"

"There's a law against breaking into people's houses."

"I thought you were squatting. You want the job or not?"

"Give me a kiss and I'll take it."

"Ron's my uncle, not my pimp."

"Who's your pimp? I'd like to talk to him."

"That's sad. That you could say something like that and think it's funny. It's kind of touching, actually."

"What's in the envelope?" I say.

"Words. You can read, right? It's a job requirement."

She walks up, dips the lollipop in the coke I left on the table and licks it.

"Be my guest," I say.

"You might want to do something about that cum stain on your shirt," she says. "It's gross."

I give Jack another weekend at the restaurant out of respect for his livelihood. He's pissed. He spits commands, I follow them, stick to my corner of the kitchen. But it's not like I'm jumping a sinking ship, business is good, it's the poker machines that are draining his coffers.

A server tells me table five wants to see me.

It happens all the time. People want to shake the hand that mashed the potatoes, sautéed the scallops, shaped those perfect little crab patties you can't get enough of. People eat with their eyes, Jack says. I'm good at this, feeding eyes, I know how to make it look pretty.

I make myself presentable, walk into the dining area.

Who's it this time? Middle-aged lawyer fucking his fresh-out-of-college paralegal? We get those a lot for some reason. City officials having a night out on the company card? We get those too. They tip for shit.

They see me before I see them.

Jiffy waves. Zoë waves.

Jack's watching how I interact with the clientele.

I smile and nod and walk over.

I ask Jiffy how he liked his venison with roasted baby potatoes, how Zoë liked her wild-caught rainbow trout with sprouts and squash.

They grin, exchange glassy looks. They're good and high.

Jiffy shakes my hand, slips me something wrapped in foil.

I pocket it, I know what it is. A gift from a friend. A little something for throwing her into his cage.

Baby gazelle in the werewolf's lair.

But then she touches his face, he smiles, and I'm thinking I did something right bringing them together without meaning to. Maybe she'll be a positive influence on him. Maybe his hands will stop shaking, he'll surprise us all and get his shit together, find a steady job, get his honor back.

"Hey, Jimmy," he says.

"Yeah?"

"Zoë says she's seen you naked."

They look at each other and start laughing.

Or he'll drag her into the sewer, reward her affection with bruises and a chipped tooth, and when people ask her she'll say it's nothing, that's what people do when they love each other, these are stamps of tough love, the only kind worth having.

Johns's house is on the other side of the railroad tracks in the Bywater, my old stomping ground before I moved into a half-shotgun with Darryl a block off of Esplanade to be closer to the Quarter. He took off three months later and left me cycling through an assortment of transient weirdo roommates until I said fuck it, I'll carry the place alone.

The Bywater days. Living hand to mouth and thinking it's romantic, heroic, reckless, it's why I came to New Orleans. I came to cut the safety lines and see which way I'd drift. I came to lose myself so I can find myself. What I found was that most of the bums in this city, the weepers and the moaners, the crazies and the druggies, the pan-handlers and dead-beats and drop-outs, they all had the same brilliant idea, same burning itch they needed to scratch. Seeing that is a kind of relief in the end. It helps you lower your expectations, feel better about dropping the bar as the years go by. You tell yourself you at least tried, the best you can do when you're surrounded by failures is to fail on your own terms, fall from grace more gracefully than the next asshole. Just don't kid yourself. Those crazy stories you think you'll tell your grandkids about living hard and dirty in the Big Easy, they've all been told and told better before you came along.

I'm thinking about all this as I pull up across from Johns's place on Poland and kill the engine. And because it's bringing me down, I switch to thinking about coincidences and statistics. Like how many times I must have walked by that green house with the peeling paint, missing boards, roof that dips like a saddle, and not know I'd one day be stalking the man who lives there.

Not stalking, I have to remind myself. Fact checking.

The old man and I must have run into each other. We stood in the same check-out line at the dirty Schwegmann's on Elysian Fields, did our laundry in the same place on St. Rock with the chipped mural-painted walls and the old soda machine that would spit out a cold drink if you nudged it the right way.

I talk myself out of a joint, I want to keep a clear head.

I pull out Ron's envelope. "Instructions," he calls them. He's typed up four single-spaced pages. How not to fuck this up for him is what it basically is, like he assumes I'm going to be a total idiot in how I go about this.

Initiate contact casually, he advises me.

Some public space with lots of foot traffic. The Rue de la Course on Magazine Street is probably best. He comes in to read the papers and have a cup of coffee. You could ask him what kind of roast he's drinking, it smells really good.

Which strikes me as a pretty lame opener.

To avoid suspicion, you'll make it seem as if you've run into him by chance on the first occasion, maybe the second one as well. I leave it to you to decide when it's safe to say things such as "Well, see you tomorrow? What time are you usually

here?" or "Want to get a *real* drink someplace?"
(FYI he's a bourbon man.)

A *real* drink? I won't be taking conversation lessons from Ron
any time soon.

Don't press too hard. Avoid personal questions
until he starts asking them himself. Use common
sense. Be tactful.

No, Mick's not right for the job, he's about as tactful as a hail-
storm. So it lands in my lap. Because I know Mick and because I'm
at the right place at the right time and because Ron likes my easy-
to-talk-to baby face. Okay, why not, I'll buy it, some things happen
that way. But Ron's a hustler, a slickster, he knows plenty of guys
who'd fact-check for half of what he's paying me. Maybe I'm not
seeing the whole picture. Maybe Mick and Ron are holding back
and Willi's been told to keep her mouth shut, suck that lollipop, act
cute, get me to play along.

Let conversations flow naturally. Allow for spon-
taneous digressions: these are often the most
fruitful source of information.

And so on.

He's given me a couple of photographs of Johns, a list of places
he likes to frequent. Morning coffee at the Rue Mondays and
Thursdays and Saturdays, flee markets Tuesdays and Sundays,
used bookstores Monday and Wednesday afternoons.

It's Monday, I could've waited for him at the Rue, Johns is a creature of habit. I tell myself I need to get a feel for his home turf,
though, his natural habitat. It'll give me an angle, something to
bring up in conversation, a hook.

But I'm full of shit. I know the Bywater like the back of my
hand. Truth is I'm a sucker for this kind of thing. I went through
a Marlowe phase in high school, read the books, watched the old

movies. I wore a fedora and my uncle's old raincoat to school. I stopped after I got beat up for it. Marlowe would have understood. He knew when to walk away. I take out Ron's manuscript. Thirty-odd pages I'm supposed to study, familiarize myself with "the project," as he calls it.

CHAPTER ONE
[DRAFT 2]

First, a few facts. Walter Johns, born August 23, 1936, in Biloxi, Mississippi, to Samuel and Nika Johns. Second of eight children, three of which died in 1929 from small pox: Darling (age 4), Sonny (age 2), and a baby girl who didn't live long enough to be named.

More facts. Walter Johns, born in February or March of 1934 in Shreveport, Louisiana; second of four children, all boys; drops out of high school in 1948, works menial jobs in Georgia and South Carolina for the next five years; picks up the saxophone around 1950; moves to New Orleans in 1968.

Still more facts: Walter Johns, born Christmas morning 1936, only child of Sonny and Nika; Sonny is killed in France in 1944; Nika remarries in 1954 or 1956, moves with her new husband to Oklahoma where she outlives him by ten years, passing away in 1982.

There is some overlap in these versions. The names Sonny and Nika come up in two out of three accounts. But is Sonny Walter's younger brother or his father? Odds are good that Nika was the name of Walter's mother. But then the second version of the so-called facts—the variant in which Walter is born in Shreveport in 1934 and has

53

three siblings, the version which gives no mention
of names—may actually be closest to the truth by
virtue of the relative scarcity of information.
The less said about a person, the less likely it
is that his or her portrait will be embellished
or fabricated.

Finally, there is a fourth version, a fourth
possible Walter Johns for us to contend with—a
Walter Johns about whom we at once know more
and less than the others. No names this time, no
fractured or fragmented genealogies, no history.
Only a snapshot, a single moment frozen in time,
arrested in space. A Walter Johns who, on one
unseasonably chilly evening in the summer of 1965,
in an alley behind a New Jersey nightclub, levels
a pistol at a kneeling man's temple and squeezes
the trigger.

This book is about all of these stories—all the
men that Walter Johns may or may not be, may or may
not have been. Or rather, it is about why we know
so little about

On and on. It's hokey.

I take out the joint, sniff it, pocket it.

I watch a small boy cycle past me, ringing the bell on his bike
over and over just to make noise the way boys do.

He spots a cat and takes off after it.

The cat tears down the street.

Reasons to run.

I grab the little black spiral notebook Willi gave me, part of the
Amateur Fact Checker Starter Kit.

I turn to page one and write

LOG

I underline it.

LOG

I turn the page and begin.

Monday, Sept. 17th
8:34 a.m.

Subject at home. Probably. Car's in the driveway
anyhow. Maybe he went out before I got here. Did
he take the bus to the Rue?

It doesn't sound right. I rip out the page and start over.

Monday, Sept. 17th
8:34 a.m.

813 Poland Avenue, Johns' house. All quiet.

Better.

I like this, I like the precision and order and cleanliness that comes with keeping a log. I even like the way the word *log* feels, what my tongue does to the roof of my mouth when I say it. I should've done this before, kept track of things.

The day I stole my first kiss.

The day I got my first dog.

The day I had my first drink, first hit of coke.

How many times I got my ass handed to me in a fight.

How many Hot Pockets I consumed in 1998.

Who won the World Series the year my father died.

Half an hour of waiting for Mongoose to come out or the boy to cycle by me with a dead cat slung over his shoulder, smoking weed with the window rolled up, deleting numbers from my cell phone, making room for order.

The Arnold twins? Delete. Fuck those fuckers.

Dusty. Delete.

Jiffy. Lon. Swede. Harry Fats. Tobias. Gone.

Who the fuck is Tobias?

I could keep doing this, deleting, purging.

But then it starts and I almost miss it.

9:07 a.m.
Johns exits house, gets in his car. I follow.

9:16 a.m.
Pulls into the Walgreens on Saint Claude and Elysian Fields.

9:22 a.m.
Exits Walgreens. I follow.

9:39 a.m.
Parks on Magazine and walks. I follow.

9:43 a.m.
The Rue. I get a cup of coffee, sit three tables away from him.
Impressions? Weathered. Withered. An old man.

10:31 a.m.
He gets a refill. I get one too.

I sit back down.

I read what I wrote.

Fuck it, I'm thinking. I'm just going to walk over there and say hello. People do it all the time, nothing weird about saying hello to someone in a coffee shop, it's the most normal thing in the world.

I reach for my mug, tip it over and spill it into my lap.

"Fucking fuck!" I say.

10:36 a.m.
He turns and looks at me. He smiles.

"You talk to him?" says Ron.

"What's that noise?" I say. "It's goddamn loud."

"Baton Rouge traffic. I'm driving. Let me shut the window."

"What's in Baton Rouge?"

"Willi didn't tell you?"

"No."

"Some people up here who used to know Walter, court records I want to look into. You just do your part. Take notes, pass it on to Willi. She's my amanuensis."

"Uh-huh."

"It means she's my assistant."

"I know what it means, Ron."

"She'll keep you from wasting your time."

"She broke into my place."

"She told me. What did Walter say?"

"He said the Saints need a new wide receiver."

He laughs.

"I didn't expect you'd get far on a first date."

"I don't think you need to worry, though, he's a talker. I'm sitting there minding my own business and the next thing I know we're buddies."

"Good. Keep him talking. You have his schedule?"

"Seared into my memory."

"So you'll be at the Rue again on Wednesday?"

"I'm a creature of habit, it's what I do on Wednesdays."

"Nothing I ought to know right away?"

"You mean like why he gave up the saxophone, where he buried the body, that sort of thing?"

"You read the first chapter. What do you think?"

"I don't get it. How do you intend to write this thing? Even if I get him to set the record straight on this or that, he's not going to dictate his life story to me from start to finish. You know that, right?"

"It doesn't bother me. You'll give me more than I have. And at this point I just need to know some things. For myself. You'll be satisfying my curiosity."

"He's not going to like your book very much."

"I can live with that."

"Anything for art?"

I hear the smile in his voice.

"Just about," he says.

D_{irt}.

I'm scrubbing off layers and layers. It's like scraping off old coats of paint, like shedding dead skin.

It feels good. I'm getting clean, getting cleansed.

My feet slosh around in standing water. I look down.

The bathtub drain is clogged. A black lump of something.

I pull it out.

Hair. Long and thick. Not mine. Not human.

I pull out strands like black spaghetti. Fistfuls of it, armfuls. I'm digging. I'm working hard.

No use. The water rises, spills over the sides of the tub.

I can't turn off the faucet. I can't breathe.

I run out of the bathroom.

I run naked into the street.

I'm knee-deep in water.

I see it's not just me, everyone's got the same problem. Thousands of busted faucets and hair-clogged drains, it's a city-wide epidemic.

No, that's not it.

Everyone plugged up their tubs and sinks, left the water running, left town in the middle of the night.

Empty streets. Abandoned homes.

Ghostville.

I start laughing. I'm laughing like a crazy person. It's the most fucked-up practical joke in history, and it's on me. I've been selected to stay behind. I've been chosen to bear witness. Except there is no one left to tell.

The water reaches my waist.

I'm laughing.

My shoulders.

I'm hoarse from laughter.

My chin.

I laugh and laugh and nothing comes out.

Banging.

A man on a roof two houses down. Black suit, white shirt, black tie, white lapel flower. Beating an upturned bucket with his walking stick.

No, with a crowbar.

It's my father.

I wave to him, glad as a pig in shit, feet stuck in mud and water seeping down my throat.

Taste of licorice. Tart and sweet.

He nods and smiles, keeps drumming, doesn't miss a beat.

"Jim!"

He drums without a break, tirelessly, courageously. He will go on and on until the end of all things that move through time.

"Jimbo!"

Because that's his job, his calling. He's been chosen to send The Signal. My father, the Chosen One. And through him I, who am his first and only son, am chosen as well. He's my father and he's working hard.

Pride wells up in me and I start to cry.

"What the fuck, Jim! You alive?"

I stumble out of bed, open the door.

Something large and red attacks my face. I fight with it.

"Whoa, whoa! What the fuck, man! You'll tear it up!"

The kite, Mick means.

"You look like shit," he says. "You ever shower?"

"You came here to ask me that?"

"Guess what we're doing today."

"I can't."

"You eat?"

Taste of licorice. Sweeter. Blood. I bit my tongue.

"Never mind, let's get some Bloody Marys. Then let's see how high this baby can fly."

"No."

"Come on, hurry up, Maggie's waiting."

O

She's good.

She tugs at the string, nudges the kite higher, leads it, guides it, coaxes it up and up.

Her first time, she says, but I don't believe it, watching her wrists, elbows, shoulders. Christ, she even puts her hips to work, swaying in the wind, waltzing on the levee. Maybe it's just how her body's built, made to make things take flight, get them off the ground and keep them up there, hovering, circling, waiting for her next command, ready to do anything, fly or fall, it's up to her.

Mick and I sit on the dew-damp grass, Maggie-watching.

The Mississippi drags like lazy sewage around the Algiers Point levee. Barges grind up and down the waterway, exhausted, disillusioned. Jet contrails crisscross the skyline, a living map of comings and goings, paling and dissolving into the blue.

I want to take a Polaroid. Because I don't trust myself to remember it right. Because I have a feeling this won't happen again. Because suddenly everything is like this, fragile and one-time-only and already rounding the bend.

Scientists say there's a lag between what is happening and what our brains tell us is happening. It's miniscule, but it's always there.

Our synapses just can't fire quick enough, we're forever living in the past. What scares us is not what tomorrow brings, but that it always comes too late.

"So," Mick says. "You fuck her yet?"

"Jesus," I say.

"You fuck her?"

"What kind of dumb question is that?"

"You'd like to fuck her, though."

"Come on, man, give it up."

"Don't fuck with me, Jimbo. Ron is easy money, I'm doing you a favor. But don't fuck with me."

Free meat. He saw her ink me. I can't blame him. Plus a hole in the gut doesn't help much with paranoia.

"You think she's got someone on the side?" I say.

He winces, spits, gives me a look I haven't seen before.

I don't like it. It makes me want to like him.

"Can't trust her, Jim."

"Maggie's not like that."

"They're all like that."

"Not Mags."

"Especially her. Watch this."

He plugs two fingers into his mouth, whistles.

She turns, looks at him. Or me. Or both of us. I can't tell from where I'm sitting.

He waves her over.

She looks up at the kite.

She lets go of the string.

It takes off, liberated.

We watch it drift out over the river, climbing the clouds, climbing up to where the air is clean and pure and there is only silence and dark empty space.

But we always fire too slow. It's already gone. It's just a ghost of a kite we're watching.

She comes over, kicks his shoe, doesn't look at me.

"What's up?" she says.

"Want to leave town?" he says. "You and me. Start over."

"Sure."

She doesn't blink.

"Where do you want to go? Want to go to Reno?"

"Yeah, Reno sounds good. Why not."

I see what he means. There's someone else. That's why she can't look me in the eye, tucks hands into pockets, watches the shrinking red dot in the sky.

Mick gives me a smirk behind her back.

"It's gone," she says. "And we never named it."

I have a thirst. I walk from bar to bar. I want to run into her and the last thing I want is to see her.

The manic laughter in Tom-All-Alone's gives me the chills.

The faces of the hard drinkers in Portnoy's are third-rate funeral parlor displays.

I walk among them.

They know me, they're glad to see me, they want to buy me shots. I let them.

Then I want to break into a church. Fucked if I know why. A hunger and a fear. Some crumbs of religious DNA swimming in my blood, some primal longing for God or something like God to be real and terrible and almighty. I want to be caught. I want to be punished. I want to be cleansed.

○

I'm pissing on the toilet seat in the men's room at Molly's because I can't come up with a good reason not to and because I can't shoot straight, and I'm thinking I want to be home for the holidays, I want to decorate a Christmas tree, I want to wrap a present for a special someone. I want someone to give me an ugly sweater.

O

I'm sacked out on Tom's couch between Tom and Andy. We're passing a finger-wide joint, doing our part to spread some joy around, the spirit of the season out of season.

"I ever tell you about the German Shepherd?" says Tom.

"I almost busted into a church tonight," I say.

"I ever tell you about it? The dog?"

"I wanted to bathe in holy water. Not dip my fingers in it, dab it on like cologne. I mean wash. Rinse and repeat. There ought to be a bulk supplier. There ought to be a holy water spring. A holy water Jacuzzi out in the desert somewhere. Imagine the goddamn line, though. You'd wait a whole lifetime for your turn and by then it would be too late, too many layers of filth to scrub off. It would never work."

"So," he says. "When they opened the gates and let us back in, which they never should've done if you ask me, and when Andy and I got back here, guess what we found?"

"Or maybe it's never too late. Maybe that's the point."

"A dog. A bitch. Dead on the couch. Right where you're sitting. Never seen her before. Don't know how she got in. We boarded up the windows, locked the door. So there's no way. You follow me? It's impossible."

"It's impossible," I say. "You're right."

"But she got in somehow. Got up on this couch and died. Man, the stink. We called but they never came to get her. With all the dead people out there, who gives a fuck about a bitch, even if she is a pure breed. Which is what Andy said she was. He knew the second he saw her. Pure German Shepherd. We buried her next to Colin. Remember Colin? Good old Colin. We've got a little cemetery going in the yard. Her tag said "Gayle Hund." "Hund" is dog in German. Right, bro? *Ein, zwei, drei.* How's the rest go?"

I look at Andy.

He's glued to the TV.

The news. A woman reporter standing next to a brick wall with graffiti on it. No, a spray-painted stencil.

Her name is Justine. I've seen her at Portnoy's a couple of times. She looks hotter on TV. That's the power of media. It increases heat.

She points to the stencil. It says

GET CLEANSED

OR BE CLEANSED

TBNO

She tells me there's been a rash of stabbings, three dead, one in critical condition. The police know more than they can say at the moment. They've got leads, hypotheses, persons of interest.

GET CLEANSED OR BE CLEANSED. A warning? A prediction? A promise? TBNO. Possibly a code. Possibly gang-related. Too early to tell, she says. Experts are working on it, a task force of linguists, cryptologists, psychologists, even a primatologist has been flown in from Dallas.

"Over to you, Carson," she says.

"Thanks, Justine. We'll keep you updated as we learn more about these gruesome murders. Tony, what's in store for us?"

A cold front is moving in, says Tony.

He shows us the map. It's true.

"How she got in is what I want to know," says Tom. "Gayle Hund. From a good family."

"Got any chips or anything?" I say.

"She just did. That's all there is to say about it. She came here to die. Gayle Hund. From a good family."

A TV commercial shows us how to lose weight and gain muscle and become the men we were meant to be.

"Everything is perpetually sliding downward," says Andy.

He looks for me when he walks in.

He sees me, smiles and waves.

I smile and wave back.

We have our table and our coffee. He buys. It's our third date and it's turning into a routine, something we can predict, something we can rely on.

"What's the word on the street?" he says.

"You know better than I do," I say.

"I'm an old man, I don't pay attention anymore. But I like to hear young men tell me. It gives me perspective."

"The world is coming to shit," I say.

He laughs.

"You told me that one last time. I want to hear something new."

"You're talking to the wrong guy," I say. "Old news is all I got, sorry."

"We'll see about that."

"See if I'm sorry?"

"See if you have nothing to say."

"Let's put money on it right now," I say.

"Let's not have you throw away your money."

I'm making big strides, we're getting chummy. He likes my face. I like how like laughs at my jokes. It's easy money.

He talks and I listen, pay attention and try to remember. Later I replay it in my head and try to pluck out the bits I think might be worth something to Ron.

He was in the Boy Scouts, he says, back in Mississippi. He was ten. He wanted to join. He wanted to wear the uniform and do the salute and get patches for merits and honorable deeds. His father called in some favors around town. The only black kid in the troop. His friends at school made him give it up. They persuaded him with fists.

His son is a musician, Lenny. Album's coming out November, they just signed a deal with Basin Street Records. He's good, better than his old man ever was. He passed on something good to his son and it blossomed in him.

Two brothers, Sonny and James. Both dead.

Owns a hardware store on Chartres in the Quarter. I've been in there dozens of times.

Played with Ollie Brixton at a late-night that went on into the morning and the following evening.

Saxophone is his thing, but he says he can "piddle" on the piano. Lots of jazz musicians are decent piano players, it's easier to compose that way, you can sound out your thoughts.

Me? Work in a restaurant. Five, six years. Sure I like it, can't complain. Except when I do.

My middle name's Dragan, after my great-grandfather.

Sushi makes me gag.

I prefer redheads but brunettes turn me on too.

I like to say *porno* instead of *porn*.

I have this pain under my ribs on the right side. Tiger Balm? Really? Why not, two billion Chinese can't be wrong.

He gets up.

"Old man's bladder. Like trying to hold water in a sock."

He goes to take a piss and it gives me a chance to log what I learned, take down some quick notes I'll expand on later.

Then I pick up the book he gave me today, *The Old Man and the Sea*. A used copy, cheap and indestructible. I open to the last page, read the last line.

The old man was dreaming about the lions.

Underlined twice with a ruler.

He comes back and brings us refills, cinnamon rolls.

"You ever been married, Jimmy?" he says.

For some reason I lie.

"Once. Long time ago."

"Can't have been that long."

"High school sweethearts. You know how it is."

"What was her name?"

"Margaret. Yours?"

"Margaret."

He smiles.

"No shit," I say.

"No shit. Where did you meet her, your Margaret?"

"New York, upstate."

"Where?"

"Oswego."

"Shit, I spent a summer there once. Hey, you ever go into Schulz's?"

"Couple of times. Yeah, sure."

"Schulz's. What a joint, man. Wow."

"Crazy good."

"Oh yeah, great place. Good burgers."

"The best."

His phone rings.

"I need to take this," he says. "My apologies."

He answers, listens.

"That's right," he says. "No."

He looks at me, smiles.

"I think so, yes. All right."

He gets up, pats me on the back.

"Got to go?"

"Got to go learn things. Young men don't tell me anything these days. They just whine about being old."

O

I walk down Magazine to my car, open the door.

"Mr. Petrovich?"

I turn. You always turn.

T-shirt and jeans. Maybe thirty. Lots of time at the gym. Tattoo sleeves. Nose that's been broken and set more than once. A bruiser. A cop.

"Yes?"

"My name is Detective Everett Hrebik, NOPD Homicide. Mind if I get in?"

"Be my guest."

He gets in the back and I get in the front. I don't know the correct protocol, if I should be craning my neck around to talk to him or face forward and look in the mirror.

"Do you want see my badge?" he says.

"Would you mind?"

He shows it to me. It's big. He lets me hold it.

"You can't be too careful," I say.

"Let's have a chat," he says.

"Here?"

He shakes his head.

"Mind driving?"

I don't mind at all, not when someone asks me nicely.

"Anywhere particular?"

"You like casinos?"

"I guess we're about to find out."

I'm plugging quarters into a poker machine at Harrah's. It swallows my money, winks at me with its flashy lights, sings to me not to give up, to hang in there, to persevere.

He likes to come here, he's not into gambling, but this is first-rate people watching. It's good training in his line of work, he says.

"What do you mean? Like looking for illegal activity?"

He scans the casino floor.

"See these people? Look at their faces. Go on, look."

I look.

They look like people's faces.

It's easy with the amateurs, he says. They hoot and holler and high-five each other. The hardened gamblers are different. Stone-cold faces, icepick eyes. Just the finger tapping on the draw button in precise little snaps. Hard to read what's going on inside. But they can't help themselves. The eyes give them away. The clenching of the jawbone. Involuntary muscle action. Microexpressions.

"Microexpressions?"

"Sounds like TV cop show bullshit, doesn't it?"

"Kind of."

"You just have to teach yourself how to look," he says.

"Clarity."

"Exactly. That's exactly right."

"Or maybe you just start seeing things. Do they still come around with free drinks in these places?"

"You're wondering why we're having this conversation."

"It's been on my mind."

"Tell me about Ron," he says.

He watches me.

I drop another quarter.

I get a combination of fruit that doesn't get along.

"I know him," I say.

"I know you do. That's why we're sitting here."

"I guess that explains it," I say.

How long have I known him?

A week. About.

How did we meet?

The party. Mick.

What is my relationship with Mick?

We work together. We cook at a restaurant.

Jack's. On Dante Street.

That's right.

How do Mick and Ron know each other?

Mick knows people. It's a small town. I have no idea.

What exactly is my relationship with Ron?

I wouldn't go so far as to call it a relationship.

I work for him, yes?

He's paying me to do something for him, talk to someone. He's writing a book.

"A thousand a week," he says. "That's pretty good money."

I look at him.

He smiles. My microexpressions are making him happy.

"A little bird told me," he says.

"Willi."

She tells him things, he says.

What kinds of things?

Things he needs to know.

About Ron?

About Ron. About me. About my relationship with Ron. My "arrangement," if I don't like to call it a relationship.

"Why? What's he done?"

Hrebik says he's going to tell me a story.

Okay, I say, but I'm out of quarters.

He pulls out his wallet and gives me a twenty.

"We'll split the proceeds," he says.

"Right down the middle."

Then he tells me a story.

Dates and names and places. Sequences of events. When I write it down later it comes out something like this:

> Detroit, March 1999.
> Ron signs a contract with a small music press for a book on Dorian Zak, the angsty heart and soul of Lawless Mindy.

> June 2000.
> The book comes out, gets good reviews. Lawless Mindy gets attention, they sign a record deal with a big label, start on a six-month coast-to-coast tour.

> Pittsburgh, August 17, 2000.
> Zak eats a fistful of pills, climbs into his hotel bathtub with his guitar, slits his wrists length-wise with an X-Acto.

> Detroit, late August 2000.
> Ron tells his agent he wants to revise the book. There's a hole in it now, it's missing a chapter, the final one, the epilogue that makes the whole

thing bigger than Zak, exemplary and tragic and
archetypal. The agent talks to the editor. The
editor talks to the publisher. The publisher takes
another look at Ron's sales figures. End of story.

New Orleans, December 2001.
Ron moves into town.

March 2002.
He starts writing for *Sound of Muzik*, begins
working on a new book.

October 2003.
He signs a contract with a local press for a biography of Damien Bolton, a.k.a. N-Zime.

February 12, 2005.
N-Zime is found in his apartment. Small-caliber
hole in the back of the head.

February 12, 2005, later that day.
Detective Everett Hrebik of NOPD Homicide is
assigned to the case. He follows leads, interro-
gates suspects, reads microexpressions.

February 14, 2005.
Hrebik calls Ron in for questioning. He's one of
the last people to be seen with N-Zime. Not a
suspect officially, a person of interest. Hrebik
gets in touch with a buddy in Detroit, who gets in
touch with Ron's old agent, who calls Hrebik and
tells him about Ron's idea for a second edition of
the Zak book.

March 2005.
A murder suspect is arrested and indicted, a man by

the name of Anton Tocqueville. Something to do with
N-Zime and Tocqueville's sister and a gambling debt.
Family honor, money, bad blood, motives galore.

June 2005.
The N-Zime book comes out, gets good press.

July 2005.
Tocqueville pleas innocent. He is convicted of
murder in the first degree. He's still on death
row.

Late July 2005.
Wilhelmina Dan moves into town.

Late August 2005.
Category Five. Everyone leaves. Everyone who can.

January 2006.
Hrebik contacts Willi. They make an arrangement.

March 2007.
Willi tells Hrebik that uncle is working on a new book,
a biography of Walter Johns, a.k.a. Mongoose. Hrebik
tries to talk his captain into taking another look at
Ron, but the NOPD is understaffed and overworked and
it's not even a cold case, it's dead and buried.

March-July 2007.
Hrebik goes it alone. He thinks Ron got away with
murder. He thinks he acquired a taste for it,
he's going to try to get his big ending again.
He keeps tabs on Ron, keeps Willi on a leash. He
approaches Johns and cautions him. Ron's been in
touch with Johns, but he's hit a wall, the old
man isn't eager to tell him stories about his

past. Ron tries a different strategy. He hires
someone to get close to Johns, slide in there
like a knife into an oyster, get him to open up.
Willi tells Hrebik and Hrebik tells the old man
to expect a guy to approach him. He even gives
him a photo of him. It's a handsome face, easy
to talk to.

"What Walter's been telling me, it's all bullshit?" I say.

"I don't know what he's been telling you."

"And you're thinking Ron did it."

"That's right."

"That he killed N-Zime."

"With a .22 caliber revolver. One shot to the base of the skull.
Precise, efficient. He wasn't in a hurry. No sign of struggle. They
knew each other."

"Is this just like a hunch or do you actually have some evidence
for this?"

"No evidence. I've been wrong before. It's possible."

"But you don't think you're wrong."

We're interrupted. Bells, lights, pandemonium.

I don't have to look. It's always some little old lady who hits the
jackpot. You strike gold just before you strike out.

"So what do you want with me?" I say. "I'm a bystander."

He wants me to keep my eyes and ears open. He wants to know
what Ron is up to. That's all, he says. For the time being.

"For the time being. What does that mean?"

"Keep doing what you're doing," he says. "Keep giving Ron what
he wants. You and Walter figure out what you want to tell him.
Stories, anecdotes, whatever keeps him interested."

"What if I say I don't want any part of this? What if I'd just rather
not get involved?"

He smiles.

"Is that what you're saying?"

"More like asking."

He looks at me.

I look at him.

He leans in.

I lean in.

He drops his voice.

I'm all ears.

"Well, then, this is the part I don't like," he says.

"Uh-huh."

"You know why I don't like it?"

I shake my head.

"No. Why?"

"Because it's the part where I have to tell you, when you do time for intent to distribute, you do heavy time."

"What do you mean?"

"The coke."

"What coke?"

"That they found in your apartment. You know, pursuant to the warrant issued this morning. Two keys, roughly. I haven't weighed it yet."

I stare at him. I can't read him.

"You're going to plant drugs on me? Are you serious?"

"Plant? No. Find. They're there right now. Want me to show you the warrant?"

His eyes are blanks.

I chill over.

Then he breaks a smile, slaps me on the shoulder.

"Jesus," he says. "Look at your face."

"I can't."

"I'm just kidding, Jimmy. I don't do threats."

"You sure?"

"I just want to help you to do the right thing. Keep me in the loop. And maybe between the two us we can prevent another murder from happening."

"And Willi."

"The three of us," he says. "We're a team."

He looks at the machine.

"How did we do?"

"We're still alive."

"Then let's cash out. We got our play time."

When I get home I check under the bed, look in the fridge, dig through the piles of dirty laundry.

Two kilos. The sick fuck. I almost wish.

I have to sit down. The pain under the ribs is on the move. It's growing restless, it wants room to breathe, explore, spelunk. I try to tell myself this is good, if it's mobile it's not committed. When it settles down again, makes its final selection, then I can start worrying. But this is good, a positive development. Psychosomatic anyway in seventy-three out of a hundred cases. Dr. K crunched the numbers himself. The stats are on my side.

I call Willi.

I just met a friend of hers, I say, we should talk.

She can't, she says, she's busy.

I tell her to unbusy herself, meet me at Three Dead Crows.

Fine, she says. She'll see me there at eight.

Right fucking now would work better for me, I say.

One hour, she says.

"You sneaky little bitch," I say.

But I've already hung up.

Hrebik's bullshit story has put the coke bug in my head.

I take out my stash, do a line.

I do another.

The primo shit I get from Mick. Works like a charm, like a dream, like a German fucking auto in overdrive.

Cloud nine at the speed of warp.

My spirits are lifted.

Clarity and light.

What good friends are for.

O

Charlie rings the bell behind the bar as I walk in.

It's not for me. Someone just bought a round for the whole place.

"Your timing is perfect," he says.

"What is it?"

"Lemon drops. I know, it's an insult to your sophisticated palate. Want it?"

"I'll drink it."

"Good boy."

Three Dead Crows is a dark hole with no windows, a ceiling you can reach up and touch from your bar stool. It's a refuge, a safe house. Federal prosecutors drinking with convicts on parole. Waitresses getting sloppy with teamsters. College professors giving college students the full college experience. You don't ask questions and you don't pass judgment. Not out loud, anyway. Leave your guns and morals at the door. Don't try to start anything or Charlie will dunk your face in the toilet. I've seen him do it.

The bell rings again.

"It's already poured," he says. "You have no choice."

"I walk the line of least resistance," I say.

"And you do it so well. You're the best walker of the least resistance line that I know of. Cheers."

"Your health, Charlie."

I notice he has a new sign up behind the bar. It says

IF YOU DON'T KNOW

WHAT "SUPERFLOUS" MEANS

YOU'RE SUPERFLOUS

He changes the TV channel from sports to news.

"I was watching that," I say.

"A man should know what's going on in the world."

"Same thing that was going on yesterday."

"You should stay informed. Where's your sense of civic duty?"

"As a matter of fact, it was called upon today."

"You don't say. How did that turn out?"

I shrug.

"To be seen?" he says.

"To be determined."

"Look at this shit," he says. "You believe this shit?"

I look at the TV.

It's Justine. She's doing her civic duty, reporting the facts, keeping me informed. She's at another murder scene, another stabbing. This homicide tour is keeping her busy.

The camera pans down her waist, down her legs, to show

GET CLEANSED

OR BE CLEANSED

TBNO

stenciled in black on the sidewalk. Marked territory.

No witnesses, she's telling me, no one saw anything, no one heard anything. There's an epidemic of blindness and deafness out there.

That's the eleventh victim so far, she says.

She says it again, eleven. A magic number. We've crossed some kind of threshold, broken through to the other side. New Orleans is back on the radar, we're making national news again. You can't keep a good city down.

The cops are getting closer, she says, they're certain now it's gang-related, drug-related.

"Fucking loons," says Charlie.

"You think so?"

"Fucking nut jobs," he says.

Billy "Boots" Wellington comes over in a disheveled blonde wig and breathes into my face. His hair grew back after the chemo, but he says he never liked it much anyway. He's got a rotating gallery of hairpieces, '80s Rocker Hair Thursdays, Rita Hayworth Fridays. Hipster kids buy him drinks and wear ironic wigs in his tribute. Make fun of him and Charlie will fuck you up.

"What do you think TBNO stands for?" Billy says. "Charlie? Hey, Jimmy? What do you think TBNO stands for?"

"I don't know," says Charlie. "What does it stand for, Billy?"

"TBNO. Two Balls Nobody Owns."

"Testicles Bring Nothing Olfactory," says Charlie.

Billy slams his fist on the bar, knocks over my drink.

"Ten Barmaids Nipples Out!"

"Sold," says Charlie.

"Fuckin' A!"

"Want me to ring the bell again?"

"Fuckin' A ring it, Charlie!"

I spot Willi walking in.

She sees me in the back, stops to talk to Charlie.

It goes on for a few minutes. She keeps me waiting.

Charlie laughs at something she says.

He leans over the bar and she kisses him on the cheek.

She gets a drink, sits next to me.

"You know Charlie?" I say. "I've never seen you in here."

"Charlie and I go way back," she says.

"You talk like you grew up together. You've only been in New Orleans two years. What is 'way back'? A week ago?"

"What is it you wanted to tell me?" she says.

"I thought you had something to tell me."

"Like?"

"Jesus, I don't know. How about the fact that Detective Hrebik of NOPD Homicide thinks your uncle is a serial killer. For starters. You know, all that stuff you didn't tell me?"

She sighs, looks at her watch.

"What exactly is your question?"

"Is Ron a goddamn sociopath? Is Hrebik out of his fucking mind? Sorry, that's two questions. Pick one and let's start there."

She stirs her drink.

"I don't know," she says.

"You don't care? How can you not care?"

"I didn't say I don't care. I said I don't know."

"He's family, isn't he?"

"Barely."

She's silent.

"Come on, give me something, Willi."

"I didn't really know him growing up," she says. "I didn't know he was in New Orleans when I moved down. I had lunch with him a few of times. He offered me a job. I needed the money, so I took it."

"And Hrebik?"

She shrugs, looks off.

"You know this case is off the books, right? There *is* no case. He's gone off the reservation. You're not obligated to help him. You can say no."

"Did you?"

"I'm just doing my civic duty."

She looks at me like I said something that might actually be true.

"He's a scary fuck," I say. "And he's dedicated. I'm talking about our friend the detective."

"He's clever," she says. "But he's not smart."

"I mean, it seems pretty bizarre, don't you think? Ron is killing the guys he's writing about so he can get the ending he wants? That's some seriously fucked-up commitment to a book."

"There is no book."

"What do you mean there is no book?"

"He's never going to finish it. It's taking him too long."

"I guess it's your job to make sure he crosses the finish line. You're his little helper, aren't you?"

She looks at me.

"Now everything is clear to you. Good."

"I'm a long way from clear."

"Maybe that's just you."

I look at her, search for traces of resemblance between uncle and niece.

"Stop doing that," she says.

"Doing what?"

"That."

I stop.

"You think he did it? You think he's capable of murder?"

"I think *you* are capable of murder. So what?"

"I asked you if you think he did it."

"And I told you. I don't know. You're doing the circles thing again."

"You're not too fond of him. Your uncle."

"Is that what you think?"

"Am I wrong?"

"You're digging. There's nothing there."

"What am I digging for that I'm not going to find?"

"Want me to say he used to touch me when I was little?"

"Did he?"

"Would it turn you on?"

"I hope not. Let's give it a try. You start."

"What if I said he stepped up when my father left, paid for my education, sends my mother a welfare check every month? She cashes it and calls me drunk to talk shit about him. How about that? Like that better?"

"Still not getting that hard-on."

She finishes her drink, gets up.

"What's Hrebik got on you, Willi? Why are you doing this?"

"Civic duty," she says. "Try using the spellchecker next time you turn in your notes. It's embarrassing."

She leaves.

I go to take a piss, stop by the poker machines. There's a cash ticket lying facedown on one of the screens.

I pick it up. It's for $0.50.

I pocket it.

More and more I'm open to signs. I watch and I listen. I receive subtle transmissions.

When I get back Billy has switched the Marilyn Monroe number for a straight-laced brunette look. He must have had it in the purse.

"Charlie! Hey, Charlie! Hey! You notice how no one ever doesn't know what time it is anymore? Everyone knows what time it is. All the fucking time. They got it all on their phones! Remember how you had to ask people when you didn't have a watch? Back in the day? They'd say *about*. *About* two o'clock. Like it was a mystery. Remember?"

Charlie puts a lemon drop in front of me.

"Mystery solved," he says.

"I can't wait."

"TBNO?"

"Uh-huh."

"Two Big Nice Ones."

"Sold."

The Rue is deserted, just Walter and me and a hipster threesome with plaid shirts and lumberjack beards knitting in the corner. We're done with the bullshit and talk straight.

"You knew from the start?" I say. "That Ron hired me?"

"Hrebik told me. Even gave me a picture of you. He didn't trust you, he wanted to see what you would do. He asked me if I'd play along, check you out, tell him what I thought."

"And?"

He smiles.

"I could tell right away."

"Tell what?"

"You're a good guy."

"That's comforting, thanks."

"You're welcome."

"What's not comforting is being the last to be told shit."

"If you're waiting to be told, you're going to be sitting there a long time."

We separate wheat from chaff, facts from stories he made up to whet my appetite, keep me coming back.

He was never in the Boy Scouts.

One brother, Sonny. Died 1999, bone cancer.

No such place as Schulz's, never been to Oswego.

Everything he said about his son is true.

His Margaret? Her name was Theodora. Teddy. I'd probably have known that much at least if I had bothered to read all the pages Ron sent me. That's what you get for skimming.

"How long were you married?" I say.

"Twenty-three years."

"What was she like?"

"She was a good woman," he says.

I wait for him to say more.

He nods at the papers on the table. I've been reading him bits from Ron's draft.

"What happens next?" he says. "Let's hear it."

I turn the page, clear my throat.

It is tempting to imagine what happens next, to give fancy free reign.

"Give fancy free reign," he says. "I like that. Go on."

Walter picks up his brother's discarded saxophone. He presses his lips against the mouthpiece. He blows. Nothing happens. The instrument is mute.

"That's good. I can't make it talk."

His fingers find the buttons. Instinctively, he presses, blows again. That's how it begins. That's also how it ends. Many years later he will stop playing as suddenly as he began: silence, then sound, then silence once more. He will not make a single recording in the meantime. For reasons that remain obscure, no audible trace will remain of the decades of music he produced between these two silences.

One is tempted to regard this symbolically: a gesture that speaks volumes about silence, as it were, speaks about all of us who come from silence and depart into silence, from and into the eternal absence of sound. But one must, I think, resist this temptation. To make the story of Mongoose's life about us is to do injustice to the man we are concerned with, to erase what is unique about him in order to reflect on what is presumably shared by everyone. And yet the shape of his life—the various intertwined and incongruous plots of his story—make it difficult not to reflect on our own stories and how they are woven into the common tapestry of humanity. Why write, why read about another human being unless it somehow relates back to us, means something to us? Why did Mongoose suddenly stop playing, stop making music, in the summer of 1976? What inspires us or compels us to choose one course of action over another, turn left instead of right? Chance? Free will? Circumstances beyond our control, but which we think we have power over? This, more than all other things, we want to know. It's why writers write, why readers read. And so again, despite our best intentions, we turn away from Mongoose to regard our own faces in the mirror. We fail to see him because we are looking at ourselves.

"That's good," he says. "It wasn't Sonny's sax, though. I found it on the street. If you can believe that. Someone threw it out. I pulled it out of a pile of trash. Man, it was in rough shape! Filthy. I put it in my mouth anyway, dumb kid. I was eight, nine."

"I like your version better."

"Been a while since I told anybody about it. It was cold. I remember my momma sent me to the corner for milk or something. I was walking back. You know, you should write that down."

"You want me to tell Ron about it?"

"Sure, let's give it to him. It'll make him happy."

"I'll say it snowed, how's that? First snow of the year. You're walking home and—"

"Snow? In Biloxi?"

"Okay, forget the snow. But it's cold as fuck. You're walking home from the store and you see something in the trash. You can't tell what it is. You're curious, you pick it up, hold it, turn it this way and that. Your fingers are stiff and the thing is cold, frozen. It hurts to hold it."

He smiles.

"Now you're talking. Go on."

"You're not sure what it is. But it seems right somehow, like you were meant to find it."

"Destiny," he says.

"And choice. You could've walked on by, but you didn't, you stopped. There's that too, right? It's not all fate."

He stares off.

Suddenly I'm alone.

He blinks, comes back.

"I made a choice," he says. "Write it down."

I write it down.

"What happens then?"

"Tell you what, Jimmy. Why don't you keep writing. Run it by me tomorrow. Let's see what you come up with on your own."

"Just make shit up?"

"You've got a knack for this. Keep it going."

"I feel like I'm being given homework."

"Something like that, yeah."

"But I've also got you, don't I?"

"Sure," he says. "Sure you got me."

He stares off again.

I look at his face. For the first time I really look.

Lines around the eyes. Wrinkles and folds and dark spots. Small scar on the left temple. Drooping old-man earlobes. A hole where he once had an earring, long ago, in another life.

"I think we've done enough for today," he says. "Old men need their naps."

"See you tomorrow?"

"Give me something good to read," he says. "And I'm still waiting for you to bring me the news, don't think I forgot."

"I'll do my best," I say.

He smiles, tired.

"That'll be just fine."

The amanuensis is efficient. I send her my notes, she proofreads and edits and preps them for Ron. The story about little Walter finding the saxophone, about paying for his first music lesson with paper delivery money, the two-week Greyhound ride from Alabama to New York, the detour in Philly that almost got him arrested on charges of possession, some of it true, some of it bullshit, a collaborative facty-fiction effort between me and Walter. Ron's a happy elf, things are really moving now, the book's coming together just the way he hoped it would.

Willi lets me buy her dinner, a steakhouse I know on Vet's with decent ribeye and all-night two-for-one drink specials on Tuesdays and Wednesdays.

She wants to sit at the bar so she can look at the TV and pretend we're not on a date.

I ask if she's met Walter, is she curious what he's like.

No and no.

How come?

What's there to know? she says. You start off with people wiping your ass for you and helping you walk, and you end with people wiping your ass for you and helping you walk.

So much for the mystery of human existence, I say. What does she do when she's not working on the book?

Taking classes at UNO.

What kind?

Acting, photography, creative writing.

What pays the rent?

She bartends.

Where?

Trey's.

How does she like it?

It's fine.

Does she mind if I ask her a personal question?

Probably. Why?

Why? Why do people want to know things about other people?

Because they don't know better. They should probably just mind their own business.

All right, different question. Should I be watching my back? What am I getting myself into?

I should always watch my back. I'm a big boy, I ought to know that by now.

Isn't she concerned? For herself?

She doesn't need a father figure, thank you.

How about a brother figure? How about a lover figure?

No and no.

Everybody needs somebody to love.

Everybody needs somebody to hate. Everybody's bitchin' cause they can't get enough. Bon Jovi. Keep the Faith. 1992.

She's good.

Oh, I have no idea.

I've got some coke at my place, weed.

My place stinks like rat. She's got class tomorrow.

"Tomorrow's just tomorrow," I say. "There's always another right after it."

"Wow," she says. "That's profound. Really, it is."

"This is a date," I say. "I'm going to walk you to your car, and then I'm going to kiss you."

"This just keeps getting better," she says.

She lets me walk her to her car.

She won't let me kiss her.

"Disappointed?" she says.

I shake my head.

"It's good to have dreams and aspirations," I say.

"That's your problem right there," she says.

I tell the woman in the university Registrar's Office I'm Willi's brother. We haven't seen each other since our father passed away four years ago. I'm in town and I want to surprise her. It's been hard for us, we've grown apart. I'm thinking of moving back to New Orleans. We need to be there for each other.

She gives me Willi's class schedule and forgets to ask for my ID.

I've got an hour to spare. I climb the levee and sit in the sun. I watch the lake and the fishermen cast their lines. No one's catching anything, but they're in high spirits. It's a good day to be out on the water and to have your friends around you.

I wait for her outside the English Department building.

She stops when she sees me, drops her head, looks pissed.

But then she comes over.

"What are you doing here?"

"Telling people I'm your brother. It's been four years since we've seen each other."

"That's disturbing."

"I know, four years is too long. Come on, let's go."

"I've got class."

"Not until tomorrow. Nine o'clock, Ceramics."

"Like I said, disturbing."

"I'll even let you drive. You have a license, don't you?"

O

I take us to City Park, pick a spot by the lake, throw down a blanket, pour wine into plastic cups. I was going to make us sandwiches, but all I found in the fridge was a jar of marinara with a thriving civilization inside and eight whole sticks of unsalted butter. I suspect I had big plans for that butter once, part of some unhappened future that I can't recall.

"Cheers," I say.

"I actually don't have time for this," she says.

"I thought we'd take the day off."

"Off what?"

"Everything."

"Good luck," she says.

I lay back, tuck my hands under my head. I watch the sky. It's a very good sky. The kind that makes you think it's true what they say, the future really is wide open, the day is what you make it. And the day after, and all the days that follow.

She leans back on her elbows, it's as far as she'll go.

She looks at me, waits for me to look back.

I close my eyes.

I feel warm cleansing light on my face.

"What?" she says.

"I didn't say anything."

"You didn't say anything? Really? You come stalk me at my school, you bring me here. Plastic cups and box wine, the full-on bullshit. So? What do you think is going to happen?"

"Nothing."

"Nothing?"

"Nothing."

"Nothing can't happen. By definition. It's what *doesn't* happen. It's simple logic."

"You're taking philosophy classes," I say. "That's good."

"Did it all just get a little too deep for you? I wouldn't want you to get a nosebleed from thinking too hard."

"It's not the thinking," I say. "It's the chemicals."

"Chemicals?"

"That they use in hospitals. To clean the floors with."

She gives me a disapproving look, turns away.

She drinks the box wine out of the plastic cup.

"You're too old for me," she says.

"How old do you think I am?"

"You own a flip phone."

"They say you're as young as you feel."

"Yeah, they say that. But you don't feel young."

"I don't?"

"Generally not. Most of the time you feel like shit."

"Not right now I don't. I feel great right now."

"Give it time," she says.

I light a joint. We smoke it.

The park has cops on cruise patrol but we're not going to get caught. Not on a day like this. We could do anything today and get away with it. We could even do nothing if we wanted to.

She passes me the joint.

"Not bad," she says.

"Gesundheit," I say.

"From Mick?"

"You know Mick?"

"Through Ron."

"The Honest Elf."

"The what?"

"He came as an elf. To the party."

She shakes her head, frowns.

"He's an asshole," she says.

"Who is?"

"Your friend Mick."

"Why do you say he's my friend?"

"Because you hang out with him. That's the company you keep. You feel like shit and you keep shit company."

"Not right now," I say. "Not at this very moment."

O

Brocato's on Carrollton is the only place in New Orleans to go for cannoli. Crispy and chewy-soft, oozing creamy goodness. You don't eat it, you get carnal with it. It's obscene.

"How's the pistachio?" I say.

"I'm not going to the movies with you," she says.

"I didn't ask you."

"We're not going to sit in the dark and hold hands."

Actually I was going to suggest a video arcade.

"Want some water?" I say.

I look for the waiter, catch his eye, raise an imaginary glass, take an imaginary sip.

She licks her spoon, squints at me.

"You're a romantic," she says.

"You make it sounds like a disease."

"It is."

"What else?"

"Certain things follow from that."

"Such as?"

"You like to think you have a sensitive soul. You like to think there's maybe a bit of a poet in you. But you don't want anyone to know you sometimes cry yourself to sleep. Because that's not very manly. And you want to be a man. It sucks being a boy."

"I thought you said I was too old for you."

"Old and mature are two different things."

"Thank you for clearing that up for me."

"What's her name?"

"Whose name?"

"The woman's. There's always a woman with guys like you."

"Is there some club I don't know I'm a part of?"

"You wear your little poetic heart on your sleeve for her, and you feel like you're getting nothing in return. But that's just what keeps you coming back for more. You can't help it. You're addicted to feeling like shit, and you think it's true love. Am I close?"

"There's no woman," I say.

She watches me play with my food. I expect her to tell me to eat it or leave it, make up my mind, I'm a full-grown man.

"You sure about that?"

"I think you need to take some more classes."

"Drop her. Find someone compatible."

"Like?"

"Gentle, soft-spoken, long-suffering. Childbearing hips. Takes your shoes off for you when you come home drunk from the bar. That kind."

"I should be writing this down. This is gold."

"You should make a checklist. I really think you've got a shot with this."

I push the bowl away.

"There's no woman."

"Whatever you need to tell yourself. Whatever works."

"That's right."

"Self-delusion. Powerful drug."

"As a matter of fact, there is someone. She's a deaf-mute. Blind too. I'm her entire world. Insanely jealous. She'd slit her wrists if she knew I was having cannoli with someone else."

"You were an only child, right? The over-inflated sense of self, it comes with being doted on. You really should've had an older brother when you were a kid."

"To steer me straight?"

"To beat the living crap out of you. It would have earned you some serious misery bragging rights down the road."

"I know you're not going to say you want to sleep with me," I say. "But we both know you want to sleep with me."

"Beat you up good and proper. Really give you something to cry about."

"It could still happen."

"Too late. It wouldn't sink in now."

She grabs her bag, gets up.

"I get this sense like we're leaving," I say.

"I'll take the bus."

"They're filthy. Have you been in one of those lately?"

"Don't you have somewhere to be?" she says. "Shouldn't you be talking to Mongoose or something? Earning your keep?"

"Walter."

"What?"

"His name is Walter."

She looks at me.

"Oh," she says.

She turns and walks away.

The waiter sets two glasses of water on the table.

"Where's your friend?" he says.

I hand him one glass, clink with him.

"Your health," I say.

Pike's not feeling good. Bloodshot eyes, vomit on the kitchen floor.

"Don't be like this, buddy," I say. "I can't afford you to be sick. How about some fresh air? Let's go for a walk. Some exercise will do us both some good."

We walk. He drags his feet.

We stop in front of the cathedral. I go in.

I light a candle. Smell of burnt wax. Stale prayers.

I sit and wait for something to happen.

I walk out untransformed.

Pike is lying on his side. He's taken a yellow liquid shit on the flagstones.

The faux gypsy fortuneteller is giving me evil looks. This isn't a one-time thing anymore, I'm a repeat offender.

I know, I know, holy ground, detritus, got it.

I dig through a trashcan, find some newspapers. They say

STABBINGS CONTINUE
TWELVE ATTACKS, TEN DEAD

I mop up Pike's shame, my shame, as best I can.
I look at her. See? I'm doing it. Okay?
She shakes her head. It's not okay. It's a long fucking ways from
okay.

We're on the back patio of Le Bon Temps, waiting for Lenny and The Closers to come on. Walter's on his first beer, I'm on my fifth and I'm telling him things I haven't told anyone in a long time. About my mother. About how we don't talk. Why I think we don't talk.

He listens, nods. He knows better than to offer advice. It's not advice I need. I need someone to listen.

He listens, but he also keeps looking around. When he sees his son, he smiles, waves him to come over. Squeezes his arm.

"This is my boy," says Walter. "My flesh and blood."

Lenny slides into the bench across from me. He gives me a look. I can tell right away we're not going to be pals.

I reach over, shake his reluctant hand.

My age. Lighter skin than his dad. Pockmarked face. Eyelashes like a girl's. Diamond stud in his ear.

"You're Ron's boy," he says.

He doesn't waste time. I like him.

"And Hrebik's too. Right?"

"And my mother's," I say.

Walter thinks it's funny.

Lenny doesn't.

"You think this is a joke?" he says.

"Easy, son," says Walter.

"Why did you bring him?" says Lenny. "Why is he here?"

"To hear you guys play. I thought you two should meet. I figured it was time."

"Yeah? Well, we've met."

"Look," I say. "Hrebik asked me to help out. That's all I'm doing here."

He smirks.

"You just want to help," he says. "I get it. You're a boy scout running around doing good deeds."

"I don't know that I'd go that far. Sounds like it takes a lot of energy."

He leans in.

"Listen, Jim. That's your name, right?"

I nod.

"I don't know what your deal is, and I don't care. But if anyone touches him, I'm holding you accountable. I'm coming to see you. You got that?"

"Lenny," says Walter.

"You understand me?" says Lenny.

"I do, yes."

"Good," he says. "As long as we understand each other."

I finish my beer.

"I think I'll be heading out," I say.

Walter sighs.

"That's not necessary," he says.

He gives Lenny a look.

Lenny stares back.

"We're all friends here," says Walter.

"Yeah," says Lenny. "Best of friends."

One of The Closers comes over to find him, they're up in five.

"Hello, Mike," says Walter. "How've you been?"

Mike looks at me. He's big. He doesn't smile.

"Doing good," he says.

"That's good. How's your momma been?"

"Doing better, thank you."

"Got to go," says Lenny.

"You coming by on Sunday?" says Walter.

"I'll see you," he says.

He walks off with Mike. They stop to talk. Mike listens. Looks over at me. Nods.

I'm meant to see this. I'm meant to take it seriously.

Walter shakes his head.

"Don't worry, he won't do anything."

"Mike looks like he might."

"Gentle as a lamb," he says.

"A very big lamb."

He sighs.

"I apologize for my son."

"No need. I get it. He's pissed. I'd be pissed."

"This thing has got him all jacked up. He thinks there's something he should be doing."

"Maybe he's right. He could be watching Ron."

"They've got him on watches, him and his boys."

"Are you serious?"

"That's what he says."

"And me? He's watching me too. I don't blame him."

"He's angry. He's restless."

He pauses.

"He knows I'm not long for this world one way or another. It scares him. Because that's something we can do nothing to remedy. That's just nature's way."

"I don't know. You look pretty sturdy to me."

He tips his hat.

"Old men take compliments wherever they can get them."

I look away and drink my beer and try to recall if I ever loved my father the way Lenny loves his. Something gets stuck in my throat. I take a swig of beer and wash it down quickly.

"I've finished my homework," I say.

He puts out his cigarette. He's picked up smoking again.

"Let's hear it," he says.

No bounce in his voice, no spark in his eye, not today.

Leonard Cohen croons from the Rue speakers, says Jesus was a sailor, all men will be sailors until the sea shall free them.

"Want to take a day off?" I say.

He shakes his head.

"I don't need a break. You're doing all the work, anyway."

"You sure?"

"What do you have?"

I open my notebook, clear my throat and say:

```
It's love at first sight. More like love at first
blow. Not because it sounds good to him, it doesn't,
it sounds terrible. But he knows this thing, he
doesn't have a name for it yet, he knows it can
```

talk, it can say things. Just not yet. He needs to
coax it, tease language out of it, make love to it.
It's rough going at first but he

I look up.

He's looking at me.

No, through me. Somewhere behind my back.

Ghosts I'll never see. Ghosts he'll never let me see.

"I'm listening," he says.

It's rough going at first, but he doesn't give up.

"It's true," he says. "That's right."

"What do you mean true? I'm making this shit up, Walter."

"It's true because you wrote it. Simple as that."

"Yeah, but you and I know it's—"

"What do we know?"

He puts his elbows on the table, leans in, looks at me.

"What do *you* know?"

Something falls away. A layer. A skin. A mask I couldn't tell was
a mask until now. Some other man is sitting in front of me. A man
with a storm raging inside. An angry man. Or a man running out
of time, afraid to die, scared to admit it. A man who knows the
next page is the last page.

"What the hell do I know?" I say.

"You know what I tell you," he says.

It's like finding a fuse and wondering what's on the other end. A
smart man would walk away. I light it.

"Why did you stop playing? Lost interest? Got bored?"

I stare at him.

He stares back.

Microexpressions? Hrebik's full of shit. People are impenetrable.

"Or did you realize you weren't that good after all?"

A softness blossoms in his face, a radiant sweetness.

"Took you a while to work up the courage to ask me."

"I didn't know if you had the stomach for it."

He smiles.

"You'd be surprised what old men can stomach."

"What's my next homework assignment?"

"Keep writing, you're doing fine."

"The boy with the saxophone, I don't know if I've got much more to say about him."

"Not much more to say, I suppose. He grew up."

"Let me take it somewhere else, really give Ron something to drool over. But you've got to promise me you won't take it the wrong way. Because this Walter I'm writing about, he's not you, so it doesn't matter what I say about him. I mean you."

"What's on your mind, Jimmy?"

"An untrue story. Fake from start to finish."

"I like it. How does it begin?"

"It begins with you standing over a dead man's body."

"And why am I doing that?"

"Because you killed him."

"How come?"

"I'm working on it."

"I hope I had a good reason," he says.

Ron's back. The Baton Rouge trip really paid off, so did the runs he made to Alexandria and Natchitoches. He says he's made a breakthrough, he wants to buy me dinner, tell me things.

I call Walter to tell him his number one fan is back in town.

He laughs.

Maybe he shouldn't be laughing, I say, maybe he should be feeling nervous instead.

He says he'll try, he doesn't want to let me down.

I call Hrebik.

He wants me to find out how far along Ron is with the book. He says it'll give us some sense of when he's planning his move. Has he talked to me about the ending? Maybe I should initiate that. But easy, we don't want to spook him.

I call Willi and tell her to meet me for drinks later.

She can't, she says, she's got an exam tomorrow.

"Come to my place and study," I say.

"No."

"Eleven?"

"No."

"I'll have the popcorn ready, you bring the lube."

○

Ron buys me dinner. He breaks up with me. It's not me, he says, it's him.

He's got it figured out, the book, the structure, the heart of the thing. He didn't see it clearly until now. It has to be the opposite of polished. It has to be brisk and raw and with jagged edges. All the pieces are there. What he needs to do is let them lie scattered, not try to make them fit neatly. They don't fit. They shouldn't. Gossip and rumors, inconsistencies and contradictions, it's what he's been after all along. Maybe I could tell as much from what he gave me to read? He's been fighting his instincts, trying to shape the story in ways it didn't want to be shaped. But now they're in sync, writer and subject, teller and tale. What I've been doing is valuable, he says, but the truth about Walter is just one of many stories about him out there. He wants the loose ends to hang loose, the seams to show.

Which is to say he doesn't need me anymore.

He asks me what I think about all this.

"I'm happy for you, Ron, don't get me wrong. But I come up a thousand dollars short. We said four grand."

"Come on, don't tell me you feel cheated. It was easy cash. And you got to meet a really interesting guy. That's worth something, isn't?"

"It's priceless."

I watch him eat, drink, use his linen napkin. He doesn't look like a killer. Write a hokey artsy book, sure. Fuck you over and never break that charming smile, absolutely. But he doesn't have the balls to pull the trigger. That's not him. That's some other guy.

"If that's what you want, fine. But I'm on to something."

"Really?"

"Pretty sure."

"What are we talking about?"

"Jersey," I say.

He grins.

"The murder. I've been down that road, nothing there. The dates don't match up, it doesn't make any sense."

"You make a big deal of it in the book. You said yourself you're curious to know certain things. This strikes me as one of those things."

He gives me a look like he thinks I'm a nice guy, I've got a handsome face, but maybe I'm getting ahead of myself thinking I understand what he wants and needs.

"What do you know about Jersey?" he says.

I shrug. We're negotiating.

He laughs.

"You're good, Jimmy. You almost had me there."

"Almost."

Dessert comes. I let the silence sit.

"He wouldn't have told you about it," he says. "He barely knows you."

"He needs to get it off his chest. I can see it. He needs to tell someone. He trusts me. And you should really try this cake, it's a miracle made out of chocolate. Here, dig in."

He takes a bite of his crème brûlée.

"You don't know what you're missing," I say.

"All right," he says. "I'm curious how far you'll be able to take this. I'll give you a week. And another grand. Deal?"

"Agreed."

We eat our respective desserts.

"So, you're almost done," I say.

He nods.

"Home stretch now."

"Congratulations."

"Yes. To both of us."

"You're giving me credit on the book cover? I hope there's a royalty check attached to that. Did we talk about portions of profits already."

He raises his glass to me, smiles.

"It's nothing but fame and fortune for you now, my lad."

Tipitina's is a giant fish tank. Big fish and little fish, fat fish and lean fish rubbing up against each other in a stew of smoke and greasy light, biting each other's slippery tails.

I swim to the bar.

Tip's isn't one of my haunts. Too far from the Quarter, my natural habitat. The bartenders don't know me here, I have to pay like everyone else. I'm anonymous, just a face in a crowd. The ground could open up and swallow me, the waters could part and close over me, and no one would notice. I was never here.

I look around for faces I know. It's what one does, one looks for familiar lines, familiar shadows.

I spot Jiffy with Zoë 9751296. He's got his hooks in her.

I don't want them to see me, I don't want to talk to them. I turn my back, spot Maggie coming up to the bar at the far end. I give all my attention to my beer bottle, start picking at the label, try to peel it off without ripping it. It's a fine art, requiring skill and planning and patience. Trick is to start from the corner and work diagonally. Take your time, don't rush. Rush and you'll fuck up.

I fuck up.

"Ain't nothin' like a sleazy bird in New Orleans," says someone behind me.

"Nothin' like it," says someone else.

Things you overhear. If I didn't suffer from laziness and a chronic failure of the imagination, I'd write a book about it. *Things You Overhear*. Which isn't a very imaginative title.

She nudges me with her shoulder.

"Hi," she says.

Black mesh top over a hot pink bra, plaid skirt, crimson suede belt with a grimacing skull buckle, knee-high leather boots, toothpick heels.

I inhale her. She smells like chemical flowers.

She nudges me again.

"Buy you a drink?"

"Mick's here?" I say.

"Why? Should he be?"

I shrug.

"It's not his kind of thing," she says.

"As long as you know what his kind of thing is."

"What's wrong?"

He whistles, she comes running. Sit, roll over, play dead. What the fuck could be wrong with that?

"Everything's peachy," I say.

I plug the beer in my mouth like a pacifier.

Someone grabs my shoulders, shakes me. The bottle knocks against a tooth. I tongue it. It's not chipped.

"Jim!"

"Tom."

He wraps his arm around my neck, breathes booze in my face.

"I tell you about the time I slept with your sister?"

"Yes."

"And you gotta tell your mom to stop calling me, man! The woman's gotta find someone her own age, it's inappropriate."

"I'll let her know, thanks."

She laughs.

I give her a look.

She shakes her head, waits for me to say something, laughs again and walks away.

"Come hang out with us," says Tom.

"Maybe later," I say.

It makes me feel better knowing she's out with him. He's a first-class degenerate, but he'll keep an eye on her, he'll make sure she goes home.

The Closers come on.

Yelps and hoots from the fishy masses.

Lenny smiles, bows. They don't waste time. They bring it hot and heavy and they don't ease up.

I look around. I'm the only one not having a good time.

What the fuck is wrong with you, Jimmy?

I don't know what's wrong with me.

Yes, you do.

Maggie.

What about her?

Leaky vessel. I pour and pour and it goes right through.

What else?

The pain under the ribs.

Legitimate concern, you'll see Dr. K tomorrow.

Zoë in Jiffyville.

You're no one's guardian angel, Jimmy, you're not qualified for the position.

I'm scared.

What scares you?

That the ground will open up and swallow me. Everything.

Stop it, Jimmy. Relax. Unclench. Sway your hips. Swing your shoulders. Nod in agreement. Smile, for fucksake.

I turn and smile at people.

They look at me and step away.

O

Half past two. Show's over.

I want to find Maggie, tell her what I've been meaning to tell her, get it off my chest and be done with it.

I scan the place, see Lenny talking to someone. But he's not paying attention to the conversation, he's watching me.

I nod, wave.

He comes over.

"Didn't think I'd see you tonight," he says.

I offer to buy him a drink. He accepts.

We smoke, drink, watch the bartenders clean up.

"Listen," he says. "The other night."

"The other night was the other night," I say.

He nods.

"If I smell something, I'll call you," I say. "If he makes a move, you'll be the first to know."

"Yeah?"

"Sure."

"How?"

"How what?"

"How are you going to call me?"

"Shit, I don't have your number. Tell me."

He tells me and I punch it in my phone.

"*Now* you can call me," he says. "Thanks for the beer."

He walks off.

Last call, says the bartender, like it's a challenge.

I look him in the eye. I'm ready for it.

Dr. K has a life-sized fluorescent skeleton hanging from a hook in his office.

"For the kids," he says.

But there are no kids, he's not a pediatrician.

He has hairy arms, a combover he keeps pawing. He inspires confidence.

"What hurts?" he says.

This and this. Sometimes this. But mostly this.

He tells me to strip, lay down, turn on my side, turn on my stomach. He prods. He listens.

He washes his hands.

I'm fine, he says, there's nothing wrong with me.

"Just like that?"

"Want me to look again?"

"You mean you didn't look thoroughly the first time?"

"And I'll look just as thoroughly the next."

"How about something for the pain?"

"You mean pills."

"I don't know. Does it come in pill form?"

He opens a drawer, shows me an assortment, a pill sampler. This is what Tom meant when he said he had a guy for me. The good doctor's a pusher, a free-market entrepreneur.

"How about these?" he says.

He points to some blue-yellow capsules.

"What are they?"

"Brand new. Just got them."

"How do I take them?"

"As needed. What about these nice little white ones? You should grab some of these greens too."

"What do they do?"

"What would you like them to do?"

The pain is real, I tell him. I thought it was just pent-up feelings, I was clenching too hard, but I was kidding myself, trying too hard to look on the bright side, stick to my new mantra. It's not in my head, it's here, under the ribcage.

He sighs, relents. Come back and piss in a cup, he says, let's take a look at your blood. Happy?

"Much obliged."

"You're a healthy man," he says. "Physically speaking."

He taps his head.

"As for up here, that's a different matter."

"Can you recommend a good shrink?"

"I don't know any good shrinks. All the shrinks I know are wankers. That's fifty bucks for the pills."

rebik calls me as I'm getting home from the doctor's.

"Just got in. Hey, you know a good shrink?"

"What?"

"Someone who's not a wanker. You cops know people, right?"

"Shut up," he says. "Turn on the news."

Easy enough when someone asks you politely.

I turn on the news.

I sit down.

Justine is telling me Mick is famous.

She's telling me Mick is dead.

He was attacked twice. First try was botched. The police didn't make the connection, there was no TBNO mark at the crime scene. They're currently looking into other murders, pieces they didn't think were part of the puzzle, expanding the scope of the investigation. They're asking us to remain calm, stick to our routines. They're encouraging us to do our civic duty, come forward with any information that would lead to arrests. They're offering cash prizes for tipoffs.

Justine tells me there's an organization out there calling itself TBNO, Take Back New Orleans. A vigilante crew taking out dealers. The police can neither confirm nor deny this, but she's got her own sources, she's way ahead of them now.

"Are you watching?" he says.

"I'm watching."

"Do you know anything about this?"

"Why do people keep asking me that?"

"When's the last time you spoke with Mick?"

"I don't know. Last week."

"You hear something, I want to know about it."

"You're working this case?"

"What's Ron been telling you?"

"He's finishing up. He says he's close."

"Did he talk about Mick to you?"

"Not recently, why?"

"I think Mick was going to do something for Ron. Ron might have to do it himself now. He might even approach you."

"What are you saying?"

"I'm saying you might find yourself propositioned."

"We don't have that kind of relationship. He doesn't trust me like that."

"Maybe he trusts you more than you think."

"And if he does? Approach me. What then?"

"Say you need time to think about it. Act surprised. Act like you didn't see it coming but maybe you could be talked into it. For the right price, why not? This is the critical stage. Don't drop the ball."

"I can't even tell what the ball is anymore."

"Eyes and ears," he says.

I feel a trickle coming out of my nose. I wipe it off.

"Lines and fucking shadows," I say.

"What?"

"Nothing."

Rock 'n' Bowl.

Boom of exploding pins. Followed by whoops and cheers.

Andy. Ballistics 101.

I find Maggie and Tom. She's crying on his shoulder.

I sit with them.

Tom looks at me.

"What the fuck," he says. "It's all fucked up, Jimmy. Everything's fucked and wrong."

I just want to sit and drink, but I know I'm obligated to say something. It's a tragic occasion, a death in the family.

"I'm sorry," I say.

Maggie wipes her eyes, shakes her head.

"You never liked him," she says.

Sympathy goes out of me like air out of a tire.

"We should've seen this coming," I say.

"We were going to get out," she says. "We were going to go to Reno, we were going to . . ."

She can't finish.

"Get cleansed?" I say.

"What? What did you say?"

"Sorry."

Tom shakes his head at me like I'm an idiot, rubs her shoulder, swallows a shot.

I decide that's about all the commiserating I can handle. I'm going to look for Andy.

He's bowling alone, winning and losing at the same time.

I stand next to a girl in a sorority shirt.

"Twelve strikes in a row!" she says. "He's amazing!"

"You should start a fan club," I say.

"And he's only got, like, three fingers!"

She's awestruck. She thinks it's hot.

"His name's Andy," I say. "Roadside bomb. Shrapnel ripped through the Humvee like cardboard. Killed two of his buddies."

"Oh my God!"

"Yeah, wow. Want to meet him? Hey, Andy! Take a break!"

He comes over.

"I'd like you to meet a fan of yours. What's your name?"

She wants to ask him things. Is he always this good? He lost his fingers in the War on Terror? That's, like, *so* brave.

Jesus holy bleeding Christ.

But I can tell he's not getting out of this, he's getting laid tonight whether he likes it or not. I've done a good deed. Some easy pussy once in a while is the least we can do for our boys in uniform.

When I get back Tom's building a pyramid out of empty shot glasses. Maggie's gone.

"You let her go? Alone?"

"Easy cowboy," he says. "She's powdering her nose."

○

I look for her in the bathroom.

"Maggie? You in here?"

She unlatches the stall, grabs my wrist, pulls me in.

Then she grabs my cock.

"Fuck me, Jimmy. Don't talk. Just fuck me."

I'd never fucked a weeping girl before. She bites my ear. The pain is searing, blinding. I come in under a minute.

She pulls down her skirt.

"I'm leaving Friday," she says. "I'm not coming back."

I give her a moment to ask me to come along.

She lights a cigarette instead.

"No use talking you out of it, I guess."

She looks at me.

"What?" I say.

"How will you remember me, Jimmy? How will you think of me when I'm gone?"

"Are you dying or just leaving town?"

She smiles.

I want to touch her face, but I know she would swat my hand away. We're past all that now.

"That day on the levee," I say. "With the kite."

She nods.

"Like that?" she says.

"Like that."

She moves and I think she's going to kiss me, but it's just her purse on the floor she wants to pick up.

"I've got to get back," she says. "Tom's waiting."

Which is when I realize that Mick was right. She's fucking someone, fine. But Tom? Of all fucking assholes? They fucking deserve each other.

O

I bang on the door until she opens.

Sleeveless shirt, panties with Disney characters. Mickey and Donald and whatshisfuckingface.

She sees the state I'm in, doesn't take the chain off.

"What do you want?"

"Let me in, Willi. I've had a shit night."

"I'm not going to fuck you. You're drunk."

"I don't want you to fuck me. Just make me a bath and put me to bed. That's all I'm asking. Will you do that for me?"

She looks at me.

"Please," I say.

She takes off the chain.

It's the sweetest thing anyone's ever done for me.

"Pike! Here, boy! Whereyat, Pike? Yo, dog!"

I find him on the kitchen floor. Tongue hanging out, blood from the mouth, blood from the anus. Head resting on an old chewed sock. Eyes closed.

Poison I bought to get rid of the rats. The smell of rats.

I was spooning a girl and he was dying.

I pick him up and carry him to the couch.

For the next six hours I scrub the bathroom, sweep and mop the floors, scour the stove, throw out everything in the fridge, do the stove again, wash the windows, dust and polish until it doesn't look like my place anymore, like someone decent and normal lives here.

I throw out the dead cactus, a birthday gift from Maggie. Because I'm prickly, she said.

I alphabetize my CDs.

I take the trash out.

I call Darryl.

"This is Darryl," says the machine.

I lay Pike in a duffel bag and put him in the trunk.

I drive in a daze.

I run a red light, get pulled over.

The cop checks out my eyes, the pupils. He sees I'm sober.

He gives me a ticket.

"Wake up," he says. "You're going get someone killed."

O

I sit on the couch with the bag in my lap and the strap in my hand. I stare at the TV with Tom and Andy. Shifting colors and shapes forming nothing I can recognize, a Rorschach test I keep failing over and over.

Tom finally asks me what's in the bag.

"My dead dog," I say.

The brothers look at each other.

"What happened?"

"I killed him," I say. "It's my fault."

"What do you want to do?"

I stare at the TV.

Tom goes into the kitchen. He comes back with sandwiches.

"Eat something," he says.

I shake my head.

He sits next to me. We watch the screen. Lines, shadows.

"Listen, Jimmy. I'm going to reach over and take that bag from you. I'm going to take him out to the yard and I'm going to bury him. You don't want me to do that, that's fine. You let me know. You don't have to say anything, just hold on to that strap. Okay?"

He takes the strap and pulls gently.

It slips out of my hand.

He takes the bag from me and gets up.

"No," I say.

He stops. He waits.

"Jimmy?"

"Where's your shovel?" I say.

○

I dig a hole next to Gayle's grave. Gayle Hund. From a good family. The miraculous German Shepherd.

I lay the bag inside and cover it with dirt.

We stand there.

"Want to say something?" Tom says.

I shake my head.

Tom turns to Andy.

"Bro?"

Andy bows his head, closes his eyes.

"Lord," he says. "Blessed be this dog, one of your own creatures. He was a good dog. He was loved. Amen."

"Amen," says Tom.

I feel drops on my face.

The sky is leaking. Low and dark and about to open up.

"Come on," Tom says.

"I'm going to stay here a bit," I say.

He takes the shovel from my hand.

"Come on, Jimmy. There's some drinking we need to do."

Ash-colored sand and mud-colored waves.
Sky boarded up with gray clouds.
The sun a fugitive on the lam.

I'm supposed to be at a funeral. Rent a black suit or see if Darryl has one, maybe work up the courage to ask Maggie if I can have one of Mick's, whichever one he's not taking with him.

So I don't.

I take the I-10 East, pick up a six-pack at gas station in Biloxi, find a spot on the beach with no footprints around.

Seagulls circle like vultures, screaming, ravenous.

I can offer them nothing, I've nothing to give.

I take off my shoes, my socks, sink my toes into the sand. Broken shells. Shards of glass slickened by the endless rolling and unrolling of the ocean.

A tiny crab circles the beer can I just emptied. It nudges it, rolls it, pushes it along. It has big plans for it.

I could take it away. Like our Lord and Savior, who giveth and taketh. Mostly taketh.

I don't want to take it away. I want to cure myself. I want to have happy childhood memories.

I have to settle for just memories.

The time my father left me in the car in an alley for three hours because he was too drunk to remember where he parked.

The time I was ten and knocked a bird's nest out of a tree with a stone. Lucky shot. The eggs shattered, tiny unborn bird fetuses spilled out. Their soft, translucent bodies. Sightless eyes, flightless limbs.

The time I called my mother a whore before I knew what the word meant. The look on her face.

If I were to keel over, if they found me lying here, taking up space, scaring off tourists, who would they call to identify me? Who would I want in the freezer room when they slide me out with a tag on my toe? Who would I want to say my name?

But they'd know better than to call anyone. It's clear as day who I am. I'm The Man of Water. I used to run in the deep and swim with the currents. Until the sea got disgusted with me and dumped me on the shore. It was many years ago.

I get up and take off my clothes.

I fold them in a pile and walk to the edge of the water.

I step in.

Knees, waist.

Chest, shoulders.

I walk through dark silt, angling an incline, going down.

The water reaches my chin.

I look back at the shore. It seems miles away.

I close my eyes and let myself go.

The black water covers me.

"Sir? Sir, wake up. You can't sleep here."

I open my eyes.

A cop.

The sky is smudged with savage reds. Morning.

Something in my mouth. A hard crumb.

I sit up, spit into my hand. Tooth fragment. I slide my tongue around, find the chipped place in the back.

"Please pick up your trash," he says.

He's young, just a kid, he's never even seen a flip phone.

I look around, count four cans. Did the crab come back for another one? Did he share the treasure with a friend?

"I had a dream," I say.

I'm standing in my living room and I'm staring at my couch. Because on the couch is my dead dog and next to him, scratching him behind the ear, is my dead father. The couch must be huge, the way things stretch out in dreams but somehow stay the same, because it's got room for more. Willi is sitting in Ron's lap. They're making out. His hand goes under her shirt. Her tongue goes in his mouth. But the strange thing is it doesn't surprise me. I realize it's all happened before, I'm watching a rerun, remembering it as I go along. I join them, I want to see what happens next, there's room on the couch for everyone. My mother comes out of the kitchen with a cake. It's for me. They sing, I blow out the candles. Maggie kisses me on the cheek. Pike barks. Andy laughs. Mick grins, puts his arm around my neck, sticks a shiv in my ribcage. He comes close and whispers in my ear. What friends are for, he says.

"Are you going to give me a ticket?" I say.

I want a ticket. It would be some kind of proof.

The cop offers me his hand.

I take it.

Our hands fit together like hands sometimes do.

He pulls me up.

"I don't feel like writing one."

"Thank you."

"You're welcome."

He smiles.

"Rough night?"

I remember a line from Hemingway, something Walter said.

"A man alone ain't got no bloody fucking chance."

He picks up a beer can, looks at it, hands it to me.

"Ain't that the truth," he says.

I dump my booze in the kitchen sink.
I flush my coke and weed down the toilet.
I make a pot of coffee.
I open a book Willi gave me, *Jazz for Beginners*, something Ron
thought I should read but I never got around to.
Miles Davis says Jazz is

```
a nigger word that white folks dropped on us.
```

The writer of the book says

```
To speak of jazz, bluntly put, is to speak of
race. While there can be no stable definition
of the musical form we call "jazz" (for it is
fundamentally mutable, inherently antagonistic
to the deadening constraints of definitions), it
is nonetheless safe to say that all conjectures,
```

theories, and speculations about the origins of jazz that neglect to take race into account miss the mark by a very wide margin. Jazz, like race, lies at the very root of what it means to be an American. Listening to jazz is a lesson in history. Understanding it better, we learn to better understand ourselves, and where we came from.

I drop on the couch, stare at the ceiling.

I get up, grab the logbook, sit at the kitchen table and turn to a fresh page. I stare at it with pen in hand.

I start to write a murder story.

He finishes reading, stands, walks out of the room. I hear him moving around in the kitchen.

"I'm having a drink," he says. "You?"

"Bourbon. Straight."

"A good bourbon makes you humble."

"Then make mine a double," I say.

He laughs.

"That's not even funny," I say.

"It's funny to me," he says. "It cracks me up."

It's my first time in his house. I don't know what I was expecting, but it's just an old man's house. Black-and-white photographs collecting dust on the walls. Piles of magazines from bygone times. Stacks of LPs by living legends and legends no one remembers. Curtains that could use washing. A wicker basket with a dozen different walking canes, though I've never seen him use one. Slippers under the bed with socks neatly folded into them. TV in the living room always on with no sound. Three cats tripping me up wherever I turn.

"So what happens next?" he says.

His voice seems to be coming under the floorboards, behind the walls. I read once somewhere about the acoustics of old Southern homes, how they were designed to carry sound, something about being able to call your slave without having to raise your voice.

"What do you mean?" I say.

"After I dump the body in the river."

"The lake. Nothing."

"What?"

"Nothing!"

"Nothing?"

I turn and he's standing behind me. He gives me a drink.

"That's it," I say. "That's the end. You dump the body. You never pick up the sax again. Except to teach Lenny."

"Your timeline is off. I kept it up until 1976."

"Okay, so you don't stop all of a sudden, you faze yourself out. As a consequence of that night."

He nods, drinks.

"Right. As a consequence."

"What, you don't like it?"

"No, that's not it, you did great. You got me convinced it really happened. But maybe it's a little too good for it's own sake."

"What do you mean?"

"Will Ron buy it? Will he believe I told you all that? If you take out some details, punch some holes in it. Maybe."

"Make it fuzzy, you mean."

"Make it more like a real memory."

"I think I can do that."

"Sure you can, you're a pro now."

He falls silent. But I feel we're not done.

"So," he says. "I murdered a man in cold blood. I put the body in the trunk. I drove down to the river."

"The lake."

"It's interesting," he says. "Interesting story."

He smiles at me.

"Wait," I say. "Hold on. Are you saying you think this is how I see you or something? You're not being serious, are you? This is just some bullshit we're serving to Ron, correct?"

He nods.

"It's just fiction," he says.

"That's right."

"It's pretty good, though."

"Thanks. I think."

"But you know," he says.

"What?"

"I wouldn't have done it that way. I wouldn't have dumped the body in the water."

"No?"

"Sounds like a lot of work. A lot of risk, too."

"Maybe you weren't thinking straight."

He shakes his head.

"I would have just left him there. That's what I'd have done. Walked away."

A cat jumps into my lap.

"Want me to change it? I can change it, I don't care, I'm not committed to it or anything."

He finishes his drink, gets up.

"Let's go stretch our legs. I need to walk. How long since you've been to a good flea market?"

I'm not overly fond of flea markets. In fact, they
creep me out. There's always newer stuff too in these places. It's
a dumping ground for rash purchases, unwanted wedding gifts
still in their boxes. But it's the sorry-looking stuff that prevails.
Umbrellas that have weathered too many storms, clocks that have
stopped caring about time, children's books with no children to be
read to, things with too much history to ever make a clean break
and start over. Leftovers on display, ruins of lives. I've had more
fun in cemeteries.

Looking for treasure is what he calls it.

I call it picking through trash. I call it touching dead people's
things.

He picks up a candleholder, looks at it, hands it to me.

It's heavy, the sort that could be good for other things too.

"That'll look good on your table," he says. "I presume you have
a table."

"I have a table."

"A man needs a place to rest his elbows," he says.

I put the candleholder back.

"I've been thinking," I say. "How about we take a break?"

"From what?"

"This. Or you take a break. I've got a handle on things. You said yourself I'm doing fine on my own."

"What you mean to say is you think I should leave town for a while. That's what Lenny thinks too."

"Maybe you should listen to him."

"You think so?"

"I do."

"Well, I guess I'm really fortunate, then."

"What do you mean?"

"I've got people giving me advice left and right. Everyone knows what's best for Walter. It's an embarrassment of riches."

"Well, fuck," I say. "What's wrong with taking good advice now and then?"

"Nothing's wrong with it."

"Especially about something like this. This is potentially serious shit. You don't know that it's not. I sure as fuck don't know."

"You cuss too much, Jimmy."

He picks up things, examines them carefully, carefully puts them back. He wants to hold them, feel their weight, feel the heft of their age in his hands.

"I'm not sure Hrebik knows what he's doing," I say.

"I thought you and the good detective were best friends."

"Aw, for fucksake."

"That dirty mouth again."

He walks back to the candleholders.

"They're a pair," he says. "Solid brass. Give them a polish and you'll see, the shine's still there."

I grind my teeth, I feel it coming. Pent up feelings. The place under the ribs where Mick shivved me.

"Shine? What the hell are you talking about, Walter? What shine?"

"The way they used to be. You can bring them back."

"You talk in circles. You play dumb."

"Do I?"

He grins.

"Why are we doing this?" I say. "Why am I doing this? For your goddamn amusement?"

He looks at me. He's listening.

"You got a death wish? Is that it? Is this just a fucking game to you? You want to see if Ron will actually do it? You know what? That's fucked up. That's some fucked up shit, man."

I'm shouting. People are looking.

I clench my fists, stare back at them.

He pulls me aside.

"Son," he says. "What is it you want to know? Why I won't run? Would *you*?"

"Fuck yes."

"But would you if you were me? Don't answer that. Because you can't. You're not me. You don't know me, Jimmy. You think you do, but you don't."

"Is that right?"

"And you don't want to, not really."

"Don't forget the money," I say. "I'm just doing it to get paid. I don't give a shit. Go on, say it. Jimmy just wants to get paid. He doesn't give a fuck."

"If Jimmy wants to be an asshole, he's got a knack for it."

"You give me homework, tell me to use my imagination, I'm a born writer. Bullshit. You tell Ron you don't want anything to do with him. Bullshit. You know what I think?"

"Tell me."

"You like the idea of someone writing a book about you. It flatters you. But you don't want to make it too easy. You're playing some fucked-up game of hide-and-seek and you've got me passing notes between you and Ron like I'm a fucking schoolgirl. I'm not stupid."

"I don't think you're stupid."

"You act like I am."

"It's you who came to me, Jimmy, remember? Working for Ron the way you've been doing, what do you think that makes you? An accomplice? Ever consider that?"

I wince in pain. I have to sit down.

An old rocking chair creaks as it receives me.

"Don't get caught looking the wrong way, Jimmy. That's all I'm saying."

"Which way is that, Walter?"

He looks at me.

"You really think I don't care if I live or die? I care a great deal. But I'm not going to run. And I'm too old to hide. That makes sense, doesn't it? You understand that, don't you?"

"You should've gone to the cops. I should've gone."

He laughs.

"Someone would fill out a form and that would be that. You think Hrebik's going to get into trouble if they find out he's been running a sideshow? A slap on the wrist, maybe. Forget him. It's you I'm worried about."

"Walter."

"Yes?"

"You're fucked up."

He smiles.

"Fair enough," he says.

He gives me a hand, pulls me up.

"Feel better?"

I nod.

"Let's find you a nice tablecloth," he says.

35

Daddy LeBlanc's. Nudity on display, just like art class. The models are jiggling their tits and sliding up and down greased poles, but the bottom line is the same.

Tom likes to tell this story about a stripper named Tease who gave blowjobs in the back room of Daddy's. She charged on a sliding scale. The longer your dick, the wider you had to open your wallet. Micropenises got freebies. Tom brags he had to dish out three hundred. The record is four-fifty, but it's a myth, he says, like Sasquatch and the Grassy Knoll shooter.

I'd ask Tease to set things straight, but she caught a dose of something quick and terminal from a Norwegian sailor and took a dive off the Algiers ferry to fast-forward things. When you know the end is nigh, take the nearest exit.

So Tom says. Which is why I think there's chance she's all right, she moved away, she became a nurse, a soccer mom, a born-again Christian. It's just that her story as Tom tells it ends the way I feel it has to. At the bottom of a dirty river, down in the sludge where no one will find her because no one will bother to look.

I put a beer in front of Hrebik, sit, take a sip of mine. Taste of unclean pipes, brews of yesteryear.

He watches the show, watches those microexpressions, honing his craft, perfecting his trade. The tits speak volumes. The asses whisper deep secrets.

I wait for him to say something.

"Walter's acting like this is some sort of a cat-and-mouse game," I say. "He needs to get out of town."

"You tried to talk him into it?"

"He's not right in the head."

He shrugs to say that's my opinion, I'm entitled to it.

I peel the label off the bottle, crumple it into a compact little ball, and flick it with my finger down the length of the bar.

I look at him.

"What?" he says.

"How exactly are you planning to pull this off? You have a plan, right? When he's ready, if he's going to do it, he's not going to announce it. He's not going to tell me about it. And he's not going to ask me to do it for him, I can tell you that. Because that would be stupid. That's not how you get away with something like this."

"Let me ask you something," he says. "How many homicides do you think go unsolved in this country? Annually."

"Can I use one of my life-lines on that?"

"Six thousand. Give or take. Six thousand people get away with murder every year. You think it's for lack of trying?"

"On the part of people like you? I don't know. Is it?"

"What would you have me do? Want to do my job for me? Be my guest. Go on, tell me. What's your idea of a good plan? I'm listening. I'm taking notes."

"I don't want to do your job."

"Willi says that Ron is leaving town for a couple of days."

"Again? He just came back."

"He got a lead, up in Lafayette. Something about Walter's old flame."

"So?"

"It gives us a window of opportunity."

"To do what?"

"Look around."

"Are you saying what I think you're saying?"

"You're looking for something to do, aren't you? Feeling antsy. Well, here you go."

"Break into his place. That's what you mean."

"I didn't say that."

"But you implied it."

"I certainly wouldn't ask you to do anything you weren't comfortable with," he says.

"I think we crossed that bridge already."

He hands me a few singles.

"We're in a strip joint. Those girls are working hard."

One of the hard-working girls sees the handoff, swirls around the pole, catapults herself in my direction.

She comes over, dances for me, turns her back, bends down.

I show my respect, tuck the money in the designated area.

She sees they're just singles, but she's a pro, she doesn't make me feel unwanted, shows me what two butt cheeks can do when they work together toward a common goal.

The dollar's strong, market analysts don't know shit.

She gives Hrebik a wave, dances over to a drooling baldy on the other side of the bar, an out-of-towner with an adhesive conference tag that says

HI! MY NAME IS
BLAIN BARKUS

Hrebik nods at the girl.

"Katya is good," he says. "Willi was better. A natural."

I look at him.

"She doesn't do it anymore," he says.

Willi giving blowjobs in the back to monster cocks, midrange dicks, micropenises. Willi blowing Hrebik because he's got something on her and she won't say what. Willi blowing Ron because he sends her mother a check every month. Tit for tat. Fair trade and no hurt feelings, no feelings to be hurt.

"You're full of shit," I say.

He laughs, wipes beer off his chin with a napkin.

"I can see why Ron picked you."

"Really? Why?"

"You're an optimist, Jimmy. You believe."

Katya is joined by another girl, a scrawny teen with a fake ID and a mother in Arkansas who's told her church group her daughter is a kindergarten teacher so many times now she practically believes it.

I get a hard-on. I don't want to, but I can't help it, I'm just meat on a stick. Meat that occasionally has a thought, a memory it drowns with liquor, a cold-sweat dream in which it flaps its limbs uselessly like a pair of featherless wings.

"I don't have this plotted out," he says. "I'm relying on you and Willi to stay alert. If you were to take the initiative to go beyond that, I'd simply want to caution you that it's not a course of action I would recommend in my official capacity."

"Which is to say?"

"Don't get caught. Don't fuck up."

"Just tell me when this is over I'll walk away clean."

"You can walk away right now," he says.

"How come I don't feel that way?"

"It could be you don't want to. You consider that? This is what you want to be doing."

He waves to the bartender for fresh beers.

"By the way, the murder story you wrote? With Walter, in Jersey?"

"Willi showed it to you?"

"Excuse me one second," he says.

He gets up and walks down to where Blain is teasing Katya with a twenty-dollar bill. He dangles it, she goes to take it, he pulls it away. He's having a good time. He's going to make her work for it.

Hrebik snaps the bill out of his hand, gives it to Katya.

Blain stands up. He says something to Hrebik.

It happens almost too quickly to see. Blaine has his arm twisted behind his back, his face shoved down hard on the bar.

Hrebik leans over and whispers to him.

Blain listens. He nods.

Hrebik whispers some more, lips almost touching Blaine's ear.

Blaine shakes his head.

Hrebik releases him.

Blain opens his wallet and gives Katya another twenty.

He looks at Hrebik.

He gives her another bill.

She blows him a kiss, turns and saunters my way.

I dig through my pockets.

Three pennies. A quarter.

A button I don't recognize.

Vicodin I got from Jiffy.

My pocketknife with the rusty blade.

She smiles at me as she walks up.

I raise my cupped hands and make my humble offering.

We're in Ron's backyard in the Garden District.
Willi on her knees with a lockpick, me keeping lookout. There's
nothing to look out for, though. A brick wall, some windows with
drawn shades on the house next door. Sunday morning, the good
people of New Orleans at the mall or in church, an auspicious hour
for breaking and entering.

"You've done this before," I say.

"You went to smart school, huh?"

"Top of my class."

"Move out of my light. And shut up. I'm trying to focus, this isn't
as easy as it looks.""

"Juvie hall, right? When?"

"There," she says.

She gets up, pushes the door open, steps in.

I stop in the doorframe.

"Cold feet?" she says.

"You believe in signs, Wilhelmina?"

"I believe you do, you can't stop talking about them. Here-a-sign, there-a-sign. In or out, make up your mind."

In.

"Only my mother calls me Wilhelmina. Shut the door."

I do as I'm told.

Ask me nicely and I'll oblige every time.

She squats.

"Snookie! Snooks! Snookster!"

Ron's cat. It slinks out of the kitchen, stops, looks at us. A stranger and a friendly.

"Hello, kitty," I say.

It scowls, hisses, scurries off.

"Don't touch anything," she says.

I look around. I want to touch. Pro-grade sound system. Rare vinyl. Things made out of silver, out of crystal and jade. Polished oak you can see your past in. Marble countertops and paintings in gilt frames. *Cigar Aficionado* and Italian shoes.

I whistle.

"Ex-wife," she says. "She left him a chunk of change. She could've taken everything, but I think it was too much for her to carry."

"The furniture, you mean?"

She looks at me.

"The money. What furniture?"

"Makes me want to get divorced."

"And if you're lucky and you pray hard, one day you will."

I pick up a crystal paperweight from the piano.

She holds her hand out.

I give it to her.

She puts it back.

"Go look in the kitchen," she says.

I look in the fridge. I make a sandwich, offer Snookie a slice of expensive-smelling cheese. It purrs, curls around my leg. Best of friends.

I hear her moving around in the next room, opening drawers.

"Find anything? Willi?"

"Keep it down," she says. "Jesus."

We're looking for clues, but we're not sure what kind. It makes looking difficult. It's not the most thought-out operation.

"Hey, did I talk you into this, or did you talk me?"

No answer.

Snookie meows at me.

"You've had enough, you little fucker."

I need to take a piss. The bathroom's so nice I decide to take a dump as well. It would be a shame to pass up a class-act opportunity like this. I sit on the can and pick up things from the sink. Shaving cream, lotion, hair gel. I open them, inhale the designer scents. Aromatic, subtle, evocative. Lavender and pine and long harbor sunsets. Lemon balm and olive oil. Summer love on the Adriatic.

I reach for the toilet paper and notice some loose sheets of yellow notepad paper on the floor behind the commode. I pick them up and read.

every biographer must ~~begin at one point~~ sooner or later come to terms with the ethical ~~consequences~~ implications of laying bare another person's life. What gives the biographer the *moral* right to disclose the most private most intimate ~~secret~~ details of ~~another's life~~ a *life not one's own?* The writer of an autobiography does not escape this question by virtue of writing ~~inwardly rather than~~ centripetally rather than centrifugally, as it were. For an autobiography is never only, or even primarily, a story about oneself. It is also a biography, a *collage* of biographies (etc etc)

On another sheet he says

anti-biography (discuss & develop—theory, genre) it wasn't until ~~an acquaintance mentioned the word in an unrelated conversation~~ I came across the word in an old newspaper from the 1930s (??) that I fully

understood the nature of my project, the genre of
the book I've been writing, the book I've been
trying to write. It would not be—it dawned on me
that it was never going to be—a standard biographical narrative——(more about) I was hunting for
the truth, trying to sort the wheat from the chaff.
I set out with the intention (so I told myself)
of being ~~honest~~ ~~sincere~~ uncompromisingly accurate.
But this is impossible. We do not possess the
language to be accurate (it's not in the *nature
of language* . . .) We alter what we observe *because*
we observe (Heisenberg) We fictionalize despite
our best intentions. But I did not give up on the
Truth. I would tell it, yes, but "tell it slant"
(E. Dickinson). And to do so, to slant it sideways,
I would first need to uncover as much as possible
(etc etc etc)

Then there's one that just says

> revise
> cross-stitch
> teasers
> HMH

HMH. How's My Honey. Hold My Hand. Hurt Me Hard. Hurt
Me Harder. I sound like Lawless Mindy.

I show it to Willi.

"It's nothing," she says. "It's garbage. He's got hundreds of these
lying around."

"Find anything good?" I say.

She shakes her head.

"I'll look in the office again," she says. "We should go."

She walks off.

"Look for what? What did we expect to find? Willi?"

My phone rings. I look at the number. Ron.

I answer it.

"Speak of the devil," I say. "How are you, Ron?"

Willi stops, walks back.

She looks at me.

I wave her off.

She gives me the finger.

"Thinking of me?" says Ron.

"Always."

"I read your notes," he says.

"Yeah?"

"Very interesting."

"I know, right?"

"He said all that to you?"

"He was a bit drunk. We both were. He just started talking. I think he finally just needed to tell someone."

"Someone like you."

"I happened to be there. I don't know if it was because of me specifically."

"Do you believe him?"

"It's not up to me to believe him or not. That's all you, Ron. I'm just giving you what he told me."

"It's fascinating."

"Crazy, yeah."

"It's bullshit."

"Like I said, you do whatever you want with it."

"No, I mean it's bullshit. You made it up."

"Why would I do that?"

"The extra grand. I give you an extension, you give me a bullshit story for a thousand bucks. Wait, that wasn't our arrangement. You were going to give me something real, weren't you? Or am I remembering this all wrong?"

"Which part?"

He laughs.

"Don't sweat it, Jimmy. You can have the money. It's a good story. I appreciate the entrepreneurial spirit. And the narrative drive of the thing. It moves really well. Which is also what gives it away, if you want to know. That and giving too many details. You needed to tone it down a bit. Solid work, though."

"Okay," I say. "Now what?"

"You collect your cash, I buy you a drink when I get back."

"I thought you said you were done, you just have to rearrange the pieces you already have."

"If you're going to provide me with fiction, I better hunt down a few facts, don't you think? And I'll use it, the story. It's too good to waste. It's got swing."

He hangs up.

"That was your uncle," I say.

"And?"

"He says I got swing."

I notice something bulging out of her jeans pocket.

"What's that?"

"None of your business."

"What is it? What did you take?"

"It belongs to me."

"You said we weren't supposed to touch anything."

"Nothing you need to worry about."

"That's reassuring. I'm feeling very reassured now."

Her phone rings. She answers it.

"Yes," she says.

She keeps her eyes on me.

"Fine," she says. "Okay. Tonight."

She puts her phone away.

"Ron?"

"I'm supposed to pay you."

"Tell me we didn't find anything here because there's nothing to find."

She rolls her eyes.

I wait.

"We didn't find anything because there's nothing to find. Okay? Anything else?"

"But you wouldn't be doing this if you didn't think there's a chance Hrebik is right."

She smirks.

"You think this is going to come back to you to bite you in the ass. Is that it? You're afraid. You're afraid this is going to end badly for you, this whole thing."

"Is it?"

"You think if he kills the old man, it'll be your fault."

"Bullshit."

"You think maybe you're giving Ron some ideas he never had to begin with. Especially this last installment you wrote. Very gruesome stuff. You need to get a grammar book, by the way."

"Don't fuck with me," I say. "I'm done being fucked with."

"You want a clean conscience. You want to be able to sleep at night, look at yourself in the mirror, bla bla, I get it. Want some advice? Drink more."

"You think what I'm worried about is how I'm going to feel at the end of the day?"

"I take it back. You're an altruist. You're doing all of this out of the goodness of your heart. Fucking spare me."

"Maybe I give a shit, Willi."

"Yeah? About what? Other than yourself, I mean."

"Walter, for instance."

"Why?"

"What do you mean why? What kind of a question is that?"

"It's simple. Why do *you* care what happens to *him*?"

"You don't? You don't give a shit if Ron kills him?"

"You didn't answer me. Why do *you* care? I'm asking you to be honest with yourself."

"And I'm asking you to fuck off."

"You're scared. You're in deep, it's too late to crawl away, and you don't want whatever happens next to be your fault. It's not about Walter. It's about you. It's about you and your guilt and what you think you can live with."

"It's sad that you should think that."

"Well, let's not linger over it or you might start crying. Or maybe what you need is a good cry. Let it all out. You'll feel better."

"I doubt it."

"You'd be surprised. You'd be surprised how quickly you can be made to feel better."

I don't trust myself to look her in the eye.

"Let's go find you an ATM," she says. "You need to get paid for all the hard work you've been doing."

37

I'm waiting on the corner and I hear Willi coming
from down the block. Her Volkswagen Rabbit coughs, chokes,
expectorates. It is a sickly creature, the offspring of Neglect and
Abuse.

"It's not going to explode," she says. "Don't look so fidgety."

"I'm not fidgety. You need to have the timing belt replaced."

"Really? You know things, huh, all about mechanics and boy
stuff? Wow."

"Don't. I'm not in the mood."

"Do you even want to come? You don't have to."

"I'm here, aren't I? We're going. You're driving. Go."

She takes us north and west onto Esplanade, driving slowly
like an old lady, peering over the wheel, mouth slightly open,
concentrating.

"This makes you nervous, doesn't it," she says. "What we're doing.
It kind of freaks you out a bit."

"No. Not at all."

"It's okay, I get it."

For once there's no sarcasm in her words.

"You probably want to get new brake pads soon."

"But first the timing belt, right?"

"Probably."

"Replaced? Huh. Sucks."

"Expensive."

She smiles.

"And who has the money these days?" she says. "What with the economy being like an old boot stuffed into a shitter, the plummeting standard of living."

"Your uncle for one."

"The Christmas elf."

"The magic man. He makes it happen."

"It?"

"Things."

"Things. Hmm. Yes. Big things, small things."

"Things upon things."

"Don't forget the Tooth Fairy," she says. "That bitch has money."

"The Tooth Fairy is fucking loaded."

She laughs.

I smile.

I'm starting to like her more than is good for me, because I'm starting to think about the future, the long game, all that big horizon shite I never got around to being good at. I'm too lazy or too stupid or it just goes against my nature. But I'm starting to think that going against my nature maybe isn't the worse thing I can contemplate doing.

"Tell me again," I say. "What's his name? What did he say?"

"Lou Smalls."

"Jesus, is that even a real name?"

"You want the short version or the long?"

"Medium rare."

Lou Smalls used to have a music joint in Metairie in the '60s, '70s, '80s. Everybody knew Lou, he was the proverbial shit back in the day. He plays Bingo Tuesdays now and gets his big-boy diapers changed by pretty nurses in a Lafayette nursing home. Lou turns put to be sharp, though, the wheels upstairs still turning. He hasn't had a hard-on since the '90s and says he isn't sure anymore what all the fuss was about anyway. He likes to talk and he likes to stroll down memory lane. Lou was low on Ron's list of contacts, a hunch, less than a lead. He trekked out there on a whim, and he hits the jackpot, he can't get the old dude to shut up.

Lou tells Ron a story. It involves a waitress and a sax player. The waitress was what you'd expect, working two jobs, saving up for college, saving for a ticket out of town. One day she meets a saxophone player. He has kind eyes, a smile that goes right to your soul. It's love. They fall for each other. But it's not going to work out for them. He has a family, a wife and a son. And she couldn't do it anyway, she would never be able to forgive herself for breaking up a happy home. They meet in hotel rooms, they part vowing never to see each other again, knowing these are empty threats, empty promises. Just when they decide to end it, when they gather the courage to really do it, she learns that she's dying. Lou can't recall what it was. He's not sure anyone really knew, something in the final stages, long past any hope of treatment. The sax player would know. She always told him everything. They leave town together. He just drops everything and leaves with her. They're gone for two months. No word, says Lou, nothing. Silence. Then he comes back. He drives her back, Lou thinks Texas, from the desert she wanted to see. He buries her in the old cemetery on Valence. There's a small funeral. Lou thinks she had some cousins in Arkansas, but no one ever heard from them.

"And the sax player?" I say. "What happens to him?"

"Goes back to his wife and kid. They reconcile. He stops playing. He goes into business with a friend and they buy a hardware store. They sell nails and carpet glue."

"So what does Ron want, confirmation?"

"We're going grave-spotting. It's right here."

She pulls up by a wrought-iron fence that runs gap-toothed and crooked around the cemetery block, cordoning off the tombs from the houses, somehow pointing out their similarities more than differences.

I take her hand. She lets me hold it. We say nothing.

We part ways at the gate. She takes the east side, I the west.

I walk by the gravestones and read the names.

Landry. Michel. Eichaker. Mueller. Here they lie.

Zeeb and Hartman. Steiner. Snakenberg and Romero-Kerner. Feuded for generations. Best of friends now.

Millaudon. Vogel. Kenny. All sipping the same wine.

"Over here," she says.

It stands alone in a corner, dropped in like an afterthought between two family graves that loom over it and cast it in perpetual shadow. The flat stone surface is wet, dank, never getting any real sun.

The writing on the stone says

JULIE DEVEREAUX

AUGUST 3, 1943

OCTOBER 27, 1976

IN LOVING MEMORY

"This is her," she says. "Julie Devereaux."

We stand there and let ourselves be silent. I take her hand again. She pulls it out.

I turn to her.

"Willi, I want to tell you something."

"Shit," she says. "Look at the date."

"What about it?"

"Look at it."

Twenty-seventh of October. It's today. She died on this day. It's her anniversary.

"Creepy. If this is one of your signs, I don't like it."

Suddenly I don't want to be there. There was a part of me that knew right away I shouldn't come, this isn't something I'm supposed to do. But she called and I wanted to see her. Maybe I also thought I needed to know, I needed to see it for myself.

Something tangible and real, non-negotiable, a stone set in a grass plot.

"Let's go," I say.

"Why? We just got here."

"We've seen what we've come to see. It's a grave. What else is there?"

"I want to take a picture."

"No."

"What do you mean no?"

"Let's just go. All right?"

She looks at me.

"No. Not all right. You want to go, go. You can find your way home."

"Why do we need a goddamn picture?"

"Because I want one. You didn't have to come, Jimmy."

She takes a picture with her phone.

"Give me that," I say.

"Fuck off."

"You're going to make me take it from you?"

"No one's making you do anything, man. Don't you get it? You're doing it all yourself. Stop blaming other people for your fucking decisions."

"Give me the phone."

"Come and take it."

"Willi."

"You don't have the balls."

She takes another picture.

"You cunt."

"That's great, that's really nice of you, thank you. Now fuck off and leave me alone."

I grab her wrist.

She doesn't kick or scratch, just frowns at me, stunned that I had the balls.

"Are you fucking kidding me?" she says.

We stop. We feel it at the same time.

Someone standing behind us. Watching us, listening.

Time passes. Ages roll by.

Then he speaks. His voice is cracked, gravely, like he just woke up, like he just stepped out of one of these tombs himself.

"Jimmy?"

It's a question. My answer is to not turn around.

Then I do, because I don't want to hear him say it again.

The dark suit hangs awkwardly from his thin shoulders. He is holding flowers, leaning on a cane. I remember it from the house, a mahogany stick with a round milky-white handle.

"What are you doing here?" he says.

He holds the flowers in front of him like he's posing for a photo, and I half expect Willi to take a take a picture with her phone and be done with it.

I look at her.

She shakes her head. I'm on my own.

I turn to him.

"I guess I'm still earning my keep," I say.

He shuffles up to me, stops.

He looks at his shoes, shakes his head.

"You don't have the right."

"How come?"

"Because I don't give you that right. This is mine. It's not yours, or Ron's, or anybody else's. You understand?"

"It's a public place."

He doesn't expect me to say that. He expected an apology and I didn't give him one. It takes him a moment to come back from that. He looks at Willi.

She looks at the ground, a sad puppy. She's right, she's too young for me, I'm too old for her. Too old for us.

"You should go," Walter says.

"We were just about to do that," she says.

She tugs at my sleeve.

I don't move.

"I'm not sure I'm ready to do that just yet," I say.

I don't know why I'm saying this. Maybe I want to see what happens next. Just simple curiosity about consequences, about the lines and shadows of things yet to be. Maybe I'm a little pissed that he didn't trust me enough to tell me about her and that I had to hear it from Willi. That an asshole like Ron knew about her before I did. Maybe I feel like he owes me this, it's something I've earned, something I mean to take.

Willi grabs my arm.

"Let's go. Now."

"Okay. You're right. You're right, we're going."

But I can't stop there. I can't just leave it at that.

"There's nothing here but some old ghosts anyway," I say.

His body slackens. He looks like he's about to collapse. He's about to crumble into ashes and be scattered by the wind.

But he doesn't. Instead he grips his cane.

He swings it up over his head. He stops.

We look at each other.

"Go on," I say.

He shakes his head.

Willi takes a step back.

"Do it," I say. "Just fucking do it already, Walter."

He brings it down quickly and I close my eyes.

○

Two hours later my head is pounding, my left eye is swollen shut, and I'm putting money in the poker machine at Three Dead Crows, slapping the draw button, betting the maximum sixteen credits. It goes up, it goes down.

I tell the ATM machine to give me more money.

It says no.

I tell Darryl's answering machine he can go fuck himself.

I tell Andy to tell Tom he can go fuck himself.

I borrow a twenty from Charlie.

My phone rings. It's Ron. I ignore it.

I put the twenty in, lose the first hand big. I look at Charlie.

He shakes his head at me and brings me a beer.

"On the house. No more loans."

"Thanks."

"That's me, I'm the house. I'm the establishment."

"I know, Charlie, you and the house are the same."

"Slow down," he says.

My phone rings again.

"Either make it shut up or answer it," he says. "This is our quiet time, people are trying to sleep."

I answer it.

"Ron. Always good to hear from you."

"How did you make out? Did you find it? Is it there?"

"Oh, yeah," I say. "I fucking found it all right."

(38)

They stole Tom Cruise's bowling shoes.

From what I hear, it was a team effort. A man alone ain't got no bloody fucking chance, but one guy standing on another's shoulders, a third keeping a lookout up on the stairs, one more watching the entrance below, that kind of collaboration restores your faith in what we can achieve if we just pitched in and worked together.

I swing, roll, gutter the ball.

I go back and sit down. It's just Andy and me. I called him and he came.

"Try to beat that," I say. "That was a beauty. I made that happen."

He takes position, aims, executes ten enemy combatants.

He comes back.

"You ever get this feeling?" I say. "Like you're watching yourself from a distance? From the other side of a mirror? Do you know what I'm talking about? Does that make any sense?"

But then I realize it's maybe not the best thing to ask a boy who came back with seven fingers and night frights.

"Don't you want to know why my face looks like this?" I say.

"If you want to tell me. Sure."

"And if I don't?"

"Then you don't."

"Thank you, Andy."

"For what?"

"For not being a dick."

He smiles.

I grab a ball, a sissy ten-pounder Andy wants me to train with.

"Slow down," he says. "Don't rush, Jimmy. Take your time. And bend."

"Bend?"

"When you enter."

I don't know what I'm supposed to enter, but I do my best to bend, which I take to mean crouch and slink a bit, like I'm a hunter, the pins are the unsuspecting prey. I'm a machine-gunner and the fuckers are just sitting out there in the open.

I take down eight.

"Well fuck me."

"Now for the tricky part," he says.

"Tell me how."

"Don't think about the gutter."

"Right, don't think about it."

"You're always thinking about the gutter, Jimmy. I can see it in your eyes, that's where you're looking."

"The gutter. It's just a place in my mind."

"No," he says. "It's real. Just don't look at it."

I roll and try my best not to look at it.

I take down one more.

One left standing, the sole survivor.

The machine sweeps him off his feet, gobbles him up, then sets them all back down together, resurrected.

"Yes," says Andy.

"Yes what?"

"I know what you mean. About the mirror and the distance."

"Andy."

"Yes?"

"How come you never talk about it? Being over there."

"The war, you mean?"

"Yes. About what happened there. What you saw."

He smiles, shakes his head.

"Jimmy. You never asked."

I'm doing prep work at Jack's and it's like I never left. He comes in the kitchen every five minutes to see if I look embarrassed enough, grateful enough, pitiful enough. I keep my head down and my mouth shut. He also knows better than to say anything. I look like I might bite.

Tom wants to know where I got the shiner. It's a beauty, he says, a prizewinner, he hasn't seen one like it in a while.

"I walked into a door."

"Big door?"

"That's right."

"Boyfriend come home?"

"That's right."

"Hate when that happens."

"Yep."

"Don't want to talk about it?"

"That's right."

He fucked my girl. He helped me bury my dog. Let's call it even.

"You should call her," he says.

"Who?"

"She's leaving town in a couple days. She's out of here. Maggie."

"That's nice. You going with her?"

"What do you mean am I going with her?"

"Are you going with her? It's a question."

"Why would I be going with her?"

"You're fucking her. It's not a huge leap in logic."

He looks at me.

"Are you out of your mind? You think I'm fucking Maggie?"

"It's okay, I don't give a shit."

"Really? You think I'm fucking Maggie? You got smacked up there harder than I thought. *You're* the one who wants to stick his dick in her, not me. You fucked her at Rock 'n' Bowl. In the goddamn toilet."

"Did she tell you that?"

"She didn't need to tell me. I'm not a complete idiot."

"Did she tell you or not?"

He shakes his head, sighs.

"Look, Jimmy. Do you like this girl or what?"

"Yes."

I say it without thinking. I think that makes it true.

"Are you sure?"

"Yes."

"Because if you're not sure, you need to make your peace with it and let it go."

"It doesn't matter either way. She's leaving."

"You're an asshole. Do you know that?"

"Why didn't she tell me she was leaving?"

"This is how she tells people she cares about. Come on, man, you know her better than I do. She wants you to make up your goddamn mind and *do* something. Or don't. And if that's what you want, then that's what you want. But I'm not fucking her. I'm her friend. You're the one she's in love with. Not that I'd want to be in your shoes. I'd much rather be standing here giving you advice, telling you you're an asshole. It works out better for me that way in the end."

"How do you know?"

"I've seen the future, I know."

"The Fields of Future Joy, the Valley of Horseshit."

"I grew up there," he says. "That's home."

O

I go out to the alley in the back. I light a cigarette.

I call her.

It rings.

I want her to pick it up. I want it to be a sign.

"This is Maggie," she says. "Don't leave a message unless you have something to say."

I hang up.

I hear the freight train coming. I wait for it to pass up on the levee across the street.

It crawls. Regulations, densely populated area.

An old engine driver hangs off the side of the locomotive, gripping the hand rail, looking up to make sure the tracks are clear of kids and afternoon drunks. It's a noble profession.

We look at each other as the engine rolls by.

He raises a hand.

I raise a hand back.

That is all.

Jack steps outside.

"You working here tonight?"

"Give a second," I say.

He goes back inside, acting more pissed than he really is. He's happy to take little stabs like this, easing us back to our comfortable level of hostility. In no time we'll hate each other as much as we always did.

I dial again.

It rings once, twice.

"It's me," I say.

"What took you so long?" says Walter.

I kick my clothes under the bed, do the dishes, scrub the john. I borrow a table from a couple across the street, cover it with the lacy sun-bleached tablecloth Walter made me buy, top it with the candleholders I've buffed and made shine. A clean ashtray. A bowl of peanuts. The place looks almost respectable.

I shower, shave, clip my nails. Almost respectable myself.

He's on time. The bell rings and I open the door.

"Jesus," he says. "You look like shit. Did I do that?"

"I think I did, actually."

He gives me something gift-wrapped.

I open it. Two long white candles.

"For the candleholders," he says.

"Thanks."

"I bought them the day Lenny was born."

I look at him.

"Are you serious? I'm not fucking lighting these."

He grins.

"Wal-Mart. Two for a dollar."

He picks up a candleholder from the table, examines it.

"Nice job."

"Thanks."

"They feel lighter."

"I didn't notice."

"You took some years off. How did that feel?"

"Good."

I put the candles in the holders. They fit snugly.

We sit and drink.

"Good bourbon," he says.

"Glad you approve."

"A man should keep a good bottle of bourbon in the house. The rest is just add-ons."

"Look," I say. "I want to apologize."

"For what?"

"For being an asshole. I crossed the line. I'm sorry."

"Forget about it."

"It's not right. I was a dick. I don't know why. I'm sorry."

"It doesn't matter."

"Yes, it does. It matters."

He looks at me.

"Jimmy, listen. We're not going to talk about it. Okay?"

"There's something else," I say. "Ron knows."

"Knows what?"

"About the cemetery. I got wasted. It'll end up in the book. He'll want to use it. It's the sort of thing he'd do. He's a parasite."

He shrugs.

"So let him use it, what's it to us?"

"If you don't care, I don't care."

"You're the one who got whacked on the skull, not me. And since we're on the topic, Hrebik's got a plan."

"What are you talking about? What plan? He didn't say anything about any plan."

The plan is this. Walter's going to get in touch with Ron. He's going to tell him he's been thinking about a lot of things lately.

He's been thinking about his life, about his past. And he's come to realize he doesn't have anything to hide. He'll say he wants to meet, start over. He's ready to talk. He'll invite him over to his house. They'll share some bourbon. They'll sit and face each other like two old adversaries at the end of a long journey. But they won't be alone. Detective Everett T. Hrebik of NOPD Homicide will be with them, hiding, waiting, watching. And when the moment comes, he'll strike.

I stare at him.

"An ambush? A fucking ambush?"

"I suppose you could call it that. I didn't think of it that way."

"Jesus Christ! Was he stoned when he came up with this? It's fucking ridiculous. It's like an idea a child might have, it's like a goddamn cartoon."

"There is often great wisdom in children."

"When is all this supposed to happen?"

"Hrebik's going to pick a date. Maybe next Saturday."

"It's a fucking joke. You're not going to do it, are you? You're not seriously considering it?"

He pours more bourbon.

I throw mine back. He sniffs his.

"He told me not to say anything, you know."

"To me?"

"Anyone. But you too, yes."

"Why? Who does he think I'm going to tell? Ron? Fuck him. Fuck them both."

"Maybe that's not why. Maybe he's trying to protect you."

"From?"

"Knowing too much. If it comes to that. If people come around asking you questions."

"If things go to shit. Like they're assured to do if we follow his idiotic plan. And Lenny? What are you telling him?"

"Lenny doesn't know. I want to keep it that way. I don't want him doing anything foolish."

"Lenny is the least foolish of the whole lot of us. He's the only one who's making any sense to me."

"I'll pass on the compliment."

"I want to be there. Saturday, whatever. I want you to call me and tell me when."

He shakes his head.

"I don't think that's a good idea."

"I don't give a shit what Hrebik says, I want to be there."

He starts to say something. But then he sighs, relents.

"If that's what you want."

"Promise me."

"Scout's honor."

"You weren't in the Scouts. Make a promise I can believe."

"How about I just give you my word?"

"That will do."

"Now get up and go get us some waters. All this serious talk is making me thirsty."

I get up, turn and look at him.

"Listen, I want to ask you something."

"Ask."

"I just want to be a good host here. I just want to share, that's all."

"Understood. You're a great host. What is it?"

"You want to do some coke?"

He smiles.

"I left that one alone a long time ago," he says.

"Got it. Sorry, I shouldn't have said anything."

"But I'll smoke some weed with you if you got it."

O

We pass a joint back and forth on the couch in silence. I leave the coke on the table in case I feel like a dip later.

I restocked from Harry Fats. Decent weed, okay coke, it's definitely a drop-off in quality since Mick. You get what you can get and you remember to be thankful.

He coughs, laughs.

"It's been a while. Stronger than I remember."

"It's all inbred varieties now. You smoked the good shit back in the day."

He nods.

"Back in the day. Shit. I'd be high for weeks. You start to forget what sober feels like anymore. You get sober and it's like another kind of high, everything so sharp and weird and at right angles."

He takes another hit.

"But this is good," he says. "This is okay."

"It's a stupid plan," I say.

He laughs.

"What, you don't think so? It's fucking stupid."

"Let me ask you something," he says. "You think Ron would want to write a book about me if I wasn't black?"

I look at him through the curtain of smoke, try to read his eyes, the lines and shadows around his eyes. It's dark outside, dark inside. We didn't turn on lights. We lit candles instead.

"What are you saying?"

"I'm asking you what you think."

"You're saying he picked you because you're black?"

"That's part of it, yeah. Oh, yeah."

"You don't believe that."

"No, no, I understand what he's doing, I do."

"What is he doing?"

"I get him. I get the kind of story he's after."

"Which is?"

"Black musicians, man."

"What about them?"

"They end badly."

"How? Why?"

"They can't hold it together. They burn too bright, they burn out too quick. You know what I'm talking about."

"I don't, actually."

"Of course you do. N-Zime was black."

"And Dorian Zak was as cracker-ass white as they get. So? It's a draw."

"That boy took his own life."

"So you're saying he's a racist. Because of N-Zime. Don't get me wrong, I'm not saying he's not a psychopath. I'm just not convinced he's a racist psychopath."

He turns and looks at me.

"Jimmy, I've seen black people take shit from white people all my life. But I don't think every white person is a racist. Believing that would make me ugly. Still, you know when your color matters to people and when it doesn't. You develop a sense for it. You can't help it."

"It never let you down? That sense?"

"You think it's as bad as prejudice?"

"I think I'm out of my depth here. I think maybe I should just shut up."

"There's prejudice and there's knowing how people are. And I don't think you should shut up. What I think you should do is pour some more bourbon out for us."

"I think I can do that and not fuck up."

He notices something on the floor, taps it with his shoe.

"Dog bowl," he says.

"Yes."

"You have a dog?"

"Used to."

He looks at me.

I drink and don't say anything.

"Don't hold on to it," he says. "It just makes it harder."

"Why did you stop playing? Can I ask? Was it the girl?"

He doesn't answer for a long time.

"I'm sorry, I shouldn't have asked."

He shakes his head.

"I got tired. It's a grind, Jimmy. I loved making music. I hated the hustle. Hard way to make a living when you got a family. You're out making money when you ought to be at home. You drink too much. You do other things too much. You wear yourself out. You start picking at the seams, and the seams come apart. You watch yourself getting older and you're still hustling, chasing the next gig, the next dollar. But that's not what people generally want to think about when they watch you play. And they shouldn't have to. Your job is to lighten the load, not add to it with your own shit. But there's a reason for all those songs about being on the road and feeling the drag of the miles, longing to be back home, forgetting where back home is. The trouble with the road is the road's got no end. It takes you places, yeah, but it takes you away from the people who matter to you most."

"Ever wonder what would have happened? If you kept going?"

He smiles, shakes his head.

"No regrets?"

"Everyone's got regrets, son. That's a curse we all share. It's just a matter of avoiding the really bad ones."

"And Lenny?"

"Lenny," he says. "What I hope for Lenny is that life will take him where life is meant to take him."

"Meaning what?"

"You know what I'm talking about. That feeling that what you're doing with your life is good and right. That it's true to who you are, deep in your core, in your bones. You're living the life you're supposed to be living. You know that feeling?"

I shake my head.

He looks at me.

"Yes, you do, you know it. It's worth fighting for, Jimmy. It's worth everything."

O

First light.

We've drunk and smoked ourselves sober.

"I'm going to bed," I say.

He nods, yawns.

"Don't drive, sleep on the couch. I'll get you some sheets."

"Much obliged," he says. "I think I will."

I go into the bedroom, start stripping the clean sheets off my bed.

"Jimmy," he says.

I come back.

"Yeah?"

"I want to apologize."

"For?"

He touches his face.

"Deserved it," I say.

"Does it hurt?"

"What doesn't?"

He smiles. He has a beautiful smile.

"You're all right," he says.

"For a white boy, you mean."

"No. You're okay."

"Scout's honor, remember? Don't forget your promise."

"Goodnight, Jimmy."

"Good morning, Walter."

A beach. Not the muddy Gulf Coast, some place with silky white sands and pearly conch shells, palm trees bending their long necks with ripe coconuts, a happy breeze running its fingers through my hair.

The boy I'm with is wearing a cop uniform. Short sleeves, short trouser legs, the NOPD Beach Collection For Kids. The badge on his chest flashes in the sun.

We're building a fort out of empty beer cans.

He sings.

> *A man alone ain't got no chance,*
> *a man alone ain't got no chance,*
> *a man alone ain't got no chance at all.*

"I taught you that one," I say.

He raises his head, smiles.

I know him.

"Andy. What are you doing here?"

We burst into laughter.

A small crab scurries into the fort.

"Welcome home," Andy says.

A black shadow descends on us. A foot comes down.

The fort is destroyed.

I look into the sun, shield my eyes. I can't see the face. There is no face, just a great black circle eclipsing the sun. The sun is collapsing, falling into itself, sinking into a dark disk rimmed with fire.

Andy starts to cry, rubs his eyes with tiny fists.

Our parents left us on the beach to play and forgot about us. We've been here for years, a whole lifetime, and we haven't grown up. No one showed us how.

"Don't cry," I say. "This is a dream, this isn't really happening."

But that's a lie. Everything you dream really happens.

I turn to the face in the sun. It's gone.

Andy's gone.

It's dark. The stars are out.

The beer cans lie crushed and useless.

I start picking them up.

"I can't camp here," I say. "I have to pick up my trash. That's what I have to do."

I turn it into a song.

$\Big(42\Big)$

Head pounding, mouth crusty and dry. Taste of licorice.

I unseal my eyes. I stare at the ceiling.

Afternoon shafts of light.

Cracks in the plaster.

Abandoned cobweb hanging in tatters by the window. I used to live with a spider and didn't know it. We shared a home. He's moved on to greener pastures, richer hunting grounds.

I find the remote under the pillow, turn on the TV, click through channels. I yawn.

Then I stop. I go back.

Justine is sitting in a bare windowless room across from a dog, a bloodhound in a black suit, white shirt, burgundy tie, his hands, weirdly human, folded over his crossed knees.

"You just said that TBNO has been active for two months," she says. "What made you decide to give an interview now?"

The dog adjusts its rubber face, turns to the camera.

He looks at me. We have an inter-species moment.

I pull the blanket up, feeling naked, exposed.

He turns to Justine and I expect him to snarl, lunge at her throat.

He doesn't, of course, he's not about to ruin that suit.

"Obviously, there has been a lot of frenetic speculation about TBNO," he says. "Mostly knee-jerk condemnation. You yourself have called us a terrorist organization."

"Which you claim not to be, correct?"

"It's a perfectly understandable reaction. It's not a label we would apply to ourselves, no. But we're not here to talk semantics. As for this conversation and why we're having it now, it's simple. We knew that we first had to get people's attention. We knew that we had to show we were serious if we wanted our message to be taken seriously."

"And what is your message?"

"Let's see if we can agree on a few things first. No sane or honest person can deny that the New Orleans Police Department is grossly inefficient, horribly mismanaged, and deeply, fatally corrupt. We don't consider this to be a matter for debate, nor is there any point in beating the proverbial dead horse here. The facts are what they are. The only question remaining is how do we address the issue. And the issue is systemic. It's rooted in the very fabric of our lives. It is this. We are afraid. We live in fear. We, you and I, we live in a city in which, according to conservative estimates, half the population does not think of dialing 911 upon witnessing a violent crime. This is a staggering statistic, a disastrous statistic. It is not a question of opinion or interpretation, then, but a simple fact of our shared existence, our shared reality, that we are living in an increasingly lawless society, a society that is collapsing around us, on the verge of disintegration."

"Anarchical times call for anarchical measures. Is that what you're saying?"

"That's not what anarchy means. Anarchy is not the same as lawlessness. Read Bakunin. Our point is that when violence has prevailed, when the legal system has been rendered ineffectual, you are left with only three options. One, you close your eyes and pretend you don't see what's happening around you. Maybe you talk yourself into believing you can't do anything about it. You're just one person, after all. What difference can one person make? It's not your job, it's not your responsibility, you've got your own problems to deal with, and so on. It's a legitimate position, of course. I think followers of Ayn Rand would have no difficulty embracing it. But if we take that route, we eventually revert back to the Hobbesian state of nature, the war of all against all. Do unto others before they do unto you. It's happening now. It's been happening here for a long time."

"What about Option Two?"

"You run. You exile yourself. From your home, your roots. Forget about this place. To hell with it. Coming back after the flood was a mistake, get out while you can and don't look back. Which is also a legitimate position. If the ship is sinking, you jump. It's simple self-preservation."

"And the third option?"

"You stand your ground. You protect your home. You try to do something. Take Back New Orleans is trying to do something."

"By murdering people."

"By targeting cancer cells."

"Drug dealers, you mean."

"Cancer cells come in many varieties."

"Can I ask you something? Have you ever personally . . ."

He cocks his head, looks amused, or exasperated, or sad, I can't tell, the rubber mask is masking his microexpressions.

"Have I killed anyone? Yes. We all have. It is a responsibility we all share."

"You are the leader?"

"I am one of the founding members."

"You call the shots. You select the targets."

"The criminals are the ones calling the shots. They select themselves by doing what they do."

"You said you have demands."

"We demand justice. It's a cliché, but it's a cliché we happen to believe in. We demand justice for the people of New Orleans. You may scoff at what I am about to say, but TBNO sees itself essentially as a humanitarian organization. You know as well as I do that there are more murders per capita in New Orleans than in any other city in the country. You make the news, you tell us these things every day. And we watch, and wait, and hope. And nothing happens. There are many good men and women who wear the NOPD uniform, people who put their lives on the line every day, not for the paltry paycheck they receive but because they are trying to do something, change something. Because they believe change is possible and it's the duty of each and every one of us to contribute to it. But they are vastly outnumbered by the criminal element on the one hand, and the corrupt officers, judges, and politicians on the other. When the rule of law is systematically being undermined by the very people entrusted to uphold it, then citizens must take the law into their own hands. Not to break it, but to honor it, protect it, make it still mean something."

"You understand that this kind of humanitarianism, as you're calling it, is morally repugnant to a lot of people."

He shrugs.

"We're not Green Peace."

"Eighteen murders so far."

He nods.

"Some of your victims had families. Children."

"What you want to say is that we're a bunch of butchers and sociopaths. And that we're fighting a losing battle."

"You think you're not?"

"There's nothing to be done, the problem is too big, too endemic, so on and so forth. It's a self-fulfilling prophecy. We're tired of it. We believe we can make a difference. We believe that me, you, all of us, can make a difference."

"By killing."

"We don't encourage others to follow our path. What we do is not for everyone."

He whips out a large knife with a serrated blade. He flips it in the air, catches the blade, offers the grip to Justine.

"Take it."

She looks at him, startled.

"Take it. Go on."

Gently this time, like he's talking to a child.

She hesitates. She takes it.

"How does it feel?"

She holds the knife.

"I don't know."

"You could say I put a weapon in your hand. You could also say I gave you an instrument, a tool. What you need to do, what everyone needs to do, is find their own tool. A petition, a picket sign, a phone call to the senator. Or you can take a camera, do what you're doing now. Your responsibility, Justine, as a journalist and as a human being, is to show us what we don't want to see. What we *need* to see, but would much rather avoid. Because it's ugly and painful to look at. It wounds our pride, and it punctures our illusions. About ourselves, about this place we call home. It's hard to look truth in the face. It's even harder when it's your own face you're being forced to look at. TBNO will do the work no one else wants to do. Until we're stopped, of course, which is going to happen sooner or later. We know the risks, we accepts the odds. We'll do what we can. It's a responsibility we refuse to back away from."

I stumble into the living room, head throbbing from the rush of blood.

"Holy crap, Walter! Did you hear any of that?"

He's slumped on the couch where I left him, head on the armrest, hands folded in his lap. Peaceful.

I go to make coffee, see that I've run out.

"Are you up? Want to go get breakfast? Or lunch? I'll drive."

No answer.

I look in. He's still sleeping.

I walk up to him, touch his shoulder.

"Walter?"

He doesn't move.

I see the cocaine on the table. The bag is almost empty.

A cold wave washes over me.

"Walter?"

I shake him.

"Hey, wake up. Come on, rise and shine, man."

I shake him again.

He lurches forward and collapses on the floor.

He lies at my feet.

I get down, touch his face. It's cold.

I get up. I turn and run into the bathroom.

I hug the toilet, retching.

I wipe my mouth, breathe.

I catch myself looking at myself in the mirror.

I slam my fist into it.

It doesn't break.

I hit it again and it cracks.

I hit it one more time and it shatters into the sink.

I pick shards out of my knuckle, wash the cuts, wrap my hand in a towel.

I go back into the living room.

I lift him up.

He's light, weightless. A vacant shell, a shriveled leaf.

I lay him down on the couch.

I fold his arms across his chest.

I get down on my knees.

We stay like that.

Then I get up.

Molly's is packed, standing room only. Everyone's wearing conference badges. A literature professors' convention. This bunch is being naughty, playing hooky in the Quarter.

"That's an old edition," says one. "It's been superseded by the Oxford."

"I used it in my seminar last year," says another. "The introduction is very thin on historical context. And some of the biographical information in the endnotes is just flat-out wrong. It's an embarrassment, really."

I walk through, pushing, scanning their tags.

PERCY WHITTAKER
UNIVERSITY OF TAMPA FL

No.

MICHELLE CASSATT
CLEMSON UNIVERSITY

No.

JAMES T. BRADSTONE
UNIVERSITY OF MICHIGAN

I walk up to him.

"You're perfect," I say.

I knock the drink out of his hand.

He's confused. The Faulkner and Melville experts around him are confused. They stop talking and stare at me. Is this some local bar custom they haven't heard about, something the travel brochures didn't mention?

"Hey, man," he says.

"I'm going to punch you in the face," I say.

"What?"

"Are you ready?"

"What?"

"I'm telling you what's going to happen. I'm telling you what your future holds. Are you ready?"

"What?"

I punch him in the jaw.

He stumbles backward, slips, goes down on his ass.

The professors pounce on me. They're not spineless wimps after all. These fuckers bench press and compete in triathlons, they're a new breed of scholar, faster, stronger, with sharper survival instincts than those fat patch-elbowed pussies they took classes from in college.

Percy has me pinned over the bar, my arm twisted behind my back.

"What the fuck are you doing! Stop! Stop it!"

He spits in my ear, snarling at me.

I elbow him in the groin.

He grunts, releases me, doubles over in pain.

Robb the bartender grabs a fistful of my hair and slams my face into the bar, splits my lip.

I surrender. I yield.

Percy lands a sneaky fist into my kidney.

"You! Back the fuck off!" says Robb.

He lowers his voice to talk to me.

"Want me to call the cops or are you going to walk away?"

I mumble into the bar.

He lets go of me.

I raise my head. I lick blood.

"I want to buy Percy a drink. I want to buy James Bradstone a drink."

"Get the fuck out, Jimmy."

"I spilled his drink and I want to buy him a new one."

"Go get yourself checked out, man. Something's not right with you."

"It's psychosomatic in most cases."

"Just fuck off."

"Yes. Yes, I think I'll fuck off now, Robb. I'm walking away. Here I am. See me? I'm walking."

The professors part in front of me. They push against each other, they don't want to catch my disease.

I step out into the light.

I cross Decatur, climb the levee, sit on a bench.

A cruise ship drifts by, a great white whale speckled with passengers like colorful scabs.

Gulls reel overhead, riding the river wind, hovering and plummeting and rising, screaming for food, screaming out of pent-up rage or pent-up grief, screaming for justice or mercy or vengeance or just for the fuck of it. You don't need a reason to scream, you need a reason not to.

The Mississippi sludges along. It knows without knowing.

A bell tinkles.

"Hey, stranger," she says.

She gets off her bike, sits next to me.

"Why haven't you called?"

"Zoë 9751296," I say.

"You've memorized it. I'm impressed. No one does that anymore."

"I always aim to make the best impression. That's the thing about me. I like to go around pleasing people. It's a humanitarian effort."

She frowns, she isn't sure what I'm saying, but she's too eager to tell me things, ask me things. What have I been up to? She hasn't seen me in art class, am I still doing that? There's a party at Daniel's tonight. Did I get an invite? She's going with Jiffy. Am I in?

A man walks by holding a little girl by the hand.

She's crying, rubbing her eyes, dragging her feet.

He yanks her wrist.

"Keep walking," he says.

I look at Zoë.

"I like your hair," I say.

I reach and touch it. I stroke it.

I grab her by the neck, pull her in and kiss her.

She struggles, stiffens, relaxes.

But I'm not really kissing her. I've suctioned my lips to hers like a scab, like one of those parasites on *Planet Nature*.

She laughs, pulls away.

I slap her across the face. It feels good.

I raise my hand again.

She jabs me in the throat with her thumb. Something from a self-defense class, maybe something Jiffy showed her.

She climbs on her bike, spits at me.

I wipe it off my cheek, lick my fingers.

"Good for you," I say.

"You fucking creep!"

I turn and watch the river.

I turn back and she's gone.

I stretch out on the bench and close my eyes. I lie there and wait for the breeze to come run its finger through my hair. I know it will. The breeze always finds me.

O

It's dusk when I wake up.

Someone tucked a dollar bill under me.

There's a bum sitting on the next bench over. An old man clutching a flask, blinking and nodding in his boozy stupor.

He looks at me, looks at the dollar in my hand.

I hold it out to him.

He shakes his head.

"No, man. It was left for you."

I tongue the cut on my lip, get the blood going again.

He offers me his flask.

I partake.

"Thank you."

He smiles, showing his bad teeth, his ravaged gums.

"Good, no?"

"Very good."

I stumble down the levee, cross Decatur without looking, get honked at and screamed at.

I go into a bar, line up shots like a firing squad, execute them one man at a time.

I build a tower out of empty shot glasses.

I'm asked to leave after it collapses.

I call the only person I can think to call.

When he picks up and I hear the clatter of plates and the shouting of orders, I remember I'm supposed to be there myself.

"Andy," I say.

"Jimmy? What's going on? Where are you?"

"It's me," I say.

"I know. You're late, man. Jack's pissed."

"I wanted to call you."

"Jimmy? Is everything okay?"

"Andy."

He's silent.

"Where are you?" he says.

"Home."

"Are you alone? Jimmy? You still there?"

"I'm sorry I called you Ghostboy."

"What are you talking about?"

"When you came back. I called you Ghostboy."

He laughs.

"Jimmy, it's okay."

"I'm sorry."

"I don't care, it's fine."

"I didn't know. I just didn't know. I'm sorry. I'm so sorry. I'm so sorry, Andy."

I'm sobbing.

"I'm so sorry. I'm so sorry. I'm so sorry."

Torn out of a notebook, folded in half, stuck to my door with a wad of chewing gum, it says

```
Jim
You haven't called and I haven't either ~~because I~~
which I think is for the best anyway. I know you'll
want to find me after you get this, but don't it
will just make things harder. Don't worry about me.
~~You know I always wanted~~ I'm leaving tomorrow and
I don't plan on coming back. I hope you'll wish me
luck. I don't know what else to say, but I couldn't
leave without saying goodbye. So goodbye Jim. Be
good to yourself. PS I left some stuff for you with
Tom. If you don't want it give it away. Just not
the record player. That's for you. ~~You're the~~
                                    Your friend
                                    Maggie
```

W e sit on the porch, drinking and smoking in the dark. He lets me be silent, lets me stare with blank eyes at the cars and the people passing by, lines and shadows coming and going in the night, leaving no trace in their wake, no mark of presence.

He pours us more bourbon. He tells me to drink.

There is a dead body in the room behind us.

I do as he says.

Then he turns and looks at me.

"I'm listening," he says.

It comes out of me garbled and looped, a twisted knot of blind alleys and do-overs. Mick and the party. The elf. The assignment. The old man. The detective. The girl. The rat poison. The murder story. The ambush plan. The four grand. The candleholders. The cocaine.

He nods as he listens. Not as a way of saying he condones or sympathizes, just that he's following me, he comprehends the meaning of my words, the sounds that emerge from me as I push the air out of my lungs and move my lips and jaw, playing my body for him like an instrument, out of tune, out of touch.

I finish. Or I just stop.

I stub out the cigarette. I wait for him to speak.

He takes a breath, nods.

"Anything else I should know?"

His eyes are clear, pupils dark and radiant. He is present. He is now and here. He's come back to us.

"Jimmy? Anything else?"

"I left it out," I say.

The thought lodged like an icepick in my side all day.

"Left what out?"

I want to shove it in deeper. I need to make it hurt more.

"The coke. I left it on the table."

He shakes his head.

"It's over. It's done."

"I left it out. I put it there. He took it."

"It's over, Jimmy."

"He wouldn't have taken it if I hadn't offered it to him. He said he didn't want any. I put it in front of him."

"You don't get to blame yourself for this. That was his choice. That was all him."

"I didn't call the cops, ambulance, anything. I walked out. I just left him there."

"He was gone. All right? He was gone and there's nothing you could have done to change that. And what you did, walking out, that's normal, that's shock."

"Shock."

"Yes. Trauma."

"Really? Trauma? Because you know what I was thinking? When I walked out and left him? Want me to tell you? I was thinking how fucked I am. When Lenny hears about this, that I killed his dad. How fucked I will be. That's what I was thinking. In my state of shock. I was thinking of myself. I was scared. I ran."

"You didn't kill anyone, Jimmy. I'd tell you if you had."

"I have to call him. I have to tell him."

"Who?"

"Lenny. I have to tell him. He has to know."

He puts a hand on my knee, looks me in the eye. He makes sure that I'm looking back at him, that we see each other.

"We're going to deal with this. I'm going to help you."

"Help me what? Help me do what, Andy?"

He leans back, gives me room to breathe.

I put my hand over my ribs.

"You all right?" he says.

Coming back to me. Settling down now. Making a nest deep inside me, a winter burrow in a dark and warm place.

"Jimmy, are you okay?"

"Yes. Yes, I'm fine."

"We're going to move him," he says.

I look at him.

"What do you mean move him? Move him where?"

"You have his keys?"

"No. I don't know. In his jacket. Why?"

"You know his house? Where it is?"

"You want to take him to his place?"

"You call the cops now, you have to explain why you waited. What took you so long. You have to explain it to them, you have to explain it to Lenny. You want to do that, fine. But if they pump him and find the drugs, that's when you're truly fucked. We need to move him. I'm going to help you."

I look at him.

"That's why you called me, isn't it?" he says.

"You don't have to do this. I'm not going to ask you to do this."

"I don't need you to ask."

He pulls something out of his pocket and gives it to me.

A white linen handkerchief.

"Your nose," he says. "You're bleeding."

O

I go down to the street, look around. It's quiet.

I turn and wave to him.

He comes out carrying the body wrapped in a blanket.

"Pop the trunk," he says.

I move to do it, then stop.

"No," I say. "In the back seat."

He gives me a look.

"Please," I say. "I don't know why. Please."

A door opens a few houses down, light spilling out into the street. Children laughing, grown-ups saying their good-byes.

"Pop the trunk," he says. "Now."

I do it.

He puts him inside and shuts it.

"How do we get there?" he says.

I stare at the trunk. I want to open it.

"Jimmy?"

I want to pull the blanket back from his face so he can breathe.

"I can drive," I say. "It's okay. I'm fine."

"We're not getting pulled over. Give me the keys."

O

He pulls up across from Walter's house, kills the engine. It's where I parked on the morning of the stakeout.

We look around. There's no one about.

I open the door to get out.

"Wait," he says.

He nods at the house.

"The lights."

I look.

"He left them on," I say.

He watches the house.

We sit and wait.

A shadow passes behind the curtains.

We look at each other.

"You sure he lives alone?"

"Yes."

The shadow passes again.

"Then who's that?"

I know him. His father's lines and shadows.

"It's Lenny," I say. "It's his son."

He paces the room. He stops, parts the curtains, peers into the dark. He's on the phone.

I sink into my seat.

"He can't see us," says Andy.

He looks up and down the street. I see him thinking.

"What?" I say.

"We have to leave him."

"Leave him where?"

"Where someone will find him."

"Like on the street? No. No fucking way. No."

The shadow stops pacing, stares at the ceiling. But there's nothing there, no answer, no voice from above.

"A park," says Andy. "On a bench."

I shake my head.

"Then you tell me," he says. "I'm listening. But if you go in there now, you're doing nothing but making it worse. So tell me. What do you want to do?"

O

The cemetery gate is locked.

"Whose grave did you say you wanted to leave him on?"

"It doesn't matter. Bad idea. I'm sorry."

"I don't know. I was thinking along the same lines."

"What do you mean?"

"Come on. Get in the car."

O

Tom opens the door and stares at us.

We walk past him, stepping over beer cans, wading through a fog of weed.

He slams the door and staggers in behind us.

"Are you fucking kidding me? Are you insane? You parked a body outside my house? Tell me you didn't park a fucking body outside my house. Jesus fucking Christ!"

Andy clears the couch of trash, shows me where to sit.

There's a nature show on TV. I've seen this one. It's about insects, shot with cutting-edge microscopic cameras.

A foot-long centipede has attached itself to the roof of a cave. It hangs down in the pitch blackness, its hungry little arms spread open, waiting. *Scolopendra gigantea*, Amazonian giant centipede. It's hunting for bats.

"I'll make coffee," says Andy.

"Fuck the coffee," says Tom. "What the fuck is going on? Jimmy? Is this for real? Are you shitting me?"

The centipede snatches one out of the air. It struggles to free itself. The predator hugs him harder, closer. I remember this part. The fucker's not going anywhere.

"I need a drink," Tom says.

"No," says Andy.

Tom blinks at him.

"What do you mean no?"

"I mean you're not having one."

Tom laughs.

"Is that what you think? You think I pay the rent around here so you can tell me what to do? Holy shit, little bro! You're out of your fucking mind if that's what you think!"

O

Tom keeps looking at the bottle on the table, but he rubs his eyes and he blows on his coffee. He lets me talk.

When I'm done, he uncorks the bottle and spikes his mug.

He spikes mine.

Andy covers his mug with his hand.

Tom turns to me.

"How much do you have left?"

196

"Left of what?"

"The money. That you got from Ron."

"I don't know. Fifteen hundred, about."

He nods, takes a sip.

Andy looks at him. He knows what Big Brother is thinking.

"Come on, Tom. We're not going to do that."

"Shut up, Andrew. You shut the fuck up now, okay?"

He turns to me.

"I'll do it. For fifteen hundred. Fair is fair. This is big shit. This goes beyond. Don't you agree?"

I nod.

"Yes," I say.

"No one else knows?"

I shake my head.

"No."

"The cop? You're going to take care of things on that end, right? He's going to be asking questions, you know that."

"I'll take care of it. It won't be a problem."

Following instructions, answering questions. I'm starting to get good at this. There's still hope. I can be trained, I can still be housebroken.

He abandons the coffee, grabs the bottle.

He salutes Andy with it, takes a pull, gives it to me.

I drink, spill, wipe my mouth with my sleeve.

"You look like shit," he says.

"I know."

"Come with the cash tomorrow. All of it."

"I can get it now."

He shakes his head.

"You're going nowhere fucked up like that. You stay here. I'll take care of it. Me and Andy. Bring it tomorrow."

He grabs my car keys from the table and gets up.

"Come on, bro," he says. "Let's finish this."

He gives Andy his hand and pulls him up to his feet.

"Tom," I say.

He turns.

"Yeah?"

"What are we after this?"

He looks at me.

"What are we?" he says.

He looks at Andy.

"We're cool," he says. "Yeah. We're brothers. We're family."

He grins.

"Thicker than water, right?"

"Right," I say.

"But Jimmy?"

"Yes?"

"Don't ever ask me to do something like this again."

"Drink this," says Tom.

I stretch out my arm, find the coffee mug without opening my eyes.

Some animals, says *Planet Nature*, go through life like this, smelling and touching and hearing only. They chose darkness over light. Cave dwellers. The Night Watch. The rejects and the misfits. Their useless eyeballs bulging behind the skin of their lids, undeveloped, pathetic. *Vestigial* is what it's called. A broken promise. A memory. A mirage.

Still, you can't miss what you never knew you didn't have. Ignorance is release. It's the knowing that fucks you.

Tom coughs, hacks. I hear him swallow.

"We got cereal. Milk should be okay. Help yourself."

I unseal my eyes.

Andy is sitting on the floor by my feet, knees pulled into his chest, watching the muted TV.

The weatherman is showing us what the future holds. He's excited. There's a cold front or hurricane or meteor coming. He shows us maps and charts. We can see for ourselves. It's approaching fast. It's almost upon us.

"Andy?"

He turns his head, unglues his eyes, looks at me.

The cobweb is back, the soft cocoon of un-presence.

He smiles.

He's gone.

He's been redeployed. He's been shipped back overnight. The PTSD Express.

No. He shipped himself back. He volunteered to return.

The desert. Homesick for a place that isn't home.

There's dirt on his arms, his face. He's been clearing minefields all night. He's been digging trenches, digging a moat around the fort.

We're protected. We're safe.

O

I walk out into the yard with my coffee.

The grass is cool and moist to my bare feet.

I stand and inhale the air with open lungs.

The dark smell of wet earth. The green smell of wet grass.

Behind them another, faint and sweet. Someone's breakfast. Eggs and ham, butter sizzling in the pan. Talk of the future over the first meal of the day. Preparations and plans, the endless hours and weeks lying open and unwritten before us.

Tom comes out, stands next to me.

He says nothing. I say nothing.

Time passes.

He nods, sniffs, grateful for the silence.

He puts a bowl of cereal on table and goes back in.

He stops at the door.

"Oh, Jack says not to come back. I tell you that already?"

"Yes."

"Fuck him, right?"

I nod. Fuck him.

The screen door slams shut.

I blow into the mug. Taste. I want sugar.

Sound of voices next-door, stepping out into the day. Time to begin again. The saying of goodbyes. The hurried repeating of plans, making of promises.

The miraculous certainty of it. The miracle of believing.

The miracle of faith.

Of prayer.

Of sacrifice.

Of ringing.

My phone.

I take it out, look at the screen.

Eleven calls. Same number. His.

I look around me. I know this place. I have been here before. The sun and the grass. The lawn chair wet from the dew. The crooked maple tree in the corner by the wire fence. The dug-over patch of earth where grass hasn't grown back yet. Pike. Gayle Hund. Love. The miracle of miracles. The Life and the Resurrection.

I have crossed the Fields of Future Joy and passed through the Valley of Horseshit, and I have come out the other side.

I have become what I am.

My thumb touches the button.

My hand brings the phone to my face.

"Lenny," I say.

Time pauses and unwinds like a spool of black string.

"Jimmy," he says. "Jesus. I've been trying to reach you. Where have you been? Why didn't you answer?"

His voice is like running water, soft, murmuring, quickened by lack of sleep.

"Have you seen Walter? Have you seen my father?"

I hear him breathing. Alive. Throbbing with life.

A miracle.

"I can't get a hold of him. Is he with you? Jimmy?"

Yes, I want to say. Yes, he is. He is with me. He will always be with me.

"Jimmy? Are you still there?"

Yes. I am.

Another miracle.

"Jimmy? Hello? Can you hear me?"

Like water running.

"Hello?"

Gentle and murmuring. Flowing into me.

I open myself to it.

Hello? Hello? Hello? Hello?

48

"Jimmy!"

Lines and shadows. Running in place.

"No," I say.

"No, I haven't seen him."

They find him in a construction dumpster on Piety, between Prieur and Roman. The stink makes a bunch of neighborhood kids climb a stepladder and look inside. The curiosity of children.

Facedown on the bricks and broken sheetrock. Arms spread like he's about to take flight. Like he fell out of the sky.

Stab wounds to the chest and throat. Flies dancing and singing to him, maggots working on him in their slow, silent way. Someone took his shoes. They forgot the wristwatch or they didn't see it. It's worth at least two grand.

He was last seen four days earlier at the Are Bar on Royal Street. Witnesses report he was in high spirits. He bought a round for the place on his way out. The patrons raised their drinks to him. The bartender rang the bell in his honor.

He was celebrating the completion of something, a book he was writing, a biography of some local musician. He was almost done, almost there. The end was in sight. He promised to come back with a signed copy. The bar has a collection of works by local writers and big-time celebrities who stop by to have their photos taken for the world-famous and internationally renowned Are Bar Writing Wall. He joked it was going to be his breakthrough, the exposure his book was going to get up there on the shelf between the well gin and the "SHUT THE FUCK RIGHT OFF" sign taped to the mirror.

I hear about it all at Three Dead Crows, Charlie shaking his head at me for the way I look, way I smell, signs telling him I'm fully and one hundred percent committed to letting myself go.

He puts a shot in front of me.

The liquid is pink, milky.

"Don't ask," he says. "It's medicinal."

I go to pay him but he waves me off.

"My money's no good?"

"Your money's fine. Problem is you don't have any."

He puts a twenty on the bar.

"Don't spend it here," he says.

"It's a bar," I say.

"I know. You're making me say shit that's bad for business."

"How do they know about the shoes?" I say.

"What shoes?"

"The guy they found. On Piety. It wasn't on the news, about the shoes."

"Ask Billy Wellington, I don't know. Catch him before he sobers up. His memory's shit when he's not drinking."

Billy grins from down the bar, his face framed by an Alice in Wonderland hairjob that makes him look sweet and menacing.

"Two grand Rolex, man! Oops! Right? Jesus, those must've been some nice fucking shoes, you know? Must've really stood out. Dumpster stenciled with the letters. TBNO, man! Twenty-two and counting! Fuckers got endurance. Not their style to loot the bodies. But those shoes must've been really nice, though."

"They wrote it with chalk," says Charlie. "They ran out of spray paint. Shit's expensive. Rough times for everyone."

"I was one day off!" says Billy. "One day, Charlie!"

Charlie shakes his head.

"Billy's taking bets. He's buying up squares on the board. You want in? I think there's a few left."

"Dollar a square," says Billy. "Guess the date, you win."

I look at him.

"He's talking about the killings," says Charlie. "Billy's into predicting the future. Gambling on death. Really good karma shit. I don't recommend it."

"You guess the date, you win," says Billy. "I think I got a Tuesday, couple of weekends open. Hey, Charlie! How much in the pot? Take a shot, Jimmy. Take a stab! No pun intended!"

He slaps the bar and laughs.

"I can't believe I broke my fist for you," says Charlie.

"The guy from Hoboken? Fuckin' A, man. Middleweight? *Bam!* More like pussyweight. Right, Charlie?"

"Where's that girl I saw you with?" says Charlie.

"Who?"

"The girl that was here. You sat right over there."

"Willi?"

"I don't know her name. She was pretty. You're too old for her."

"She said you were friends."

He shrugs.

"Look around. Everyone's my friend."

"Hey, Charlie! Put me down for another square! Where's the board? Here, put me down for five. No, four. Four for me and one for Jimmy."

"That's all the money you got, Billy."

"I got a good feeling about this one. I had my palm read the other day."

"Yeah? What's it say?"

"Tide's about to turn, man. I'm on an upswing."

November 8, 2007
9:30 a.m.

Hrebik, Everett. Detective, NOPD Homicide.
Petrovich, James D. Unemployed.

Where have I been?
Around. Nowhere. Looking for work.
Why haven't I called him?
I didn't know I was supposed to call.
I didn't know?
No.
Pause.
I watch the news?
I try.
Am I fucking with him?
No. Yes. Yes, I saw it.

When did I last talk to Ron? When did I last talk to Willi?

I tell him when.

And Walter?

Thursday.

Where?

Same place. Coffee shop.

Did anything happen? Anything out of the ordinary?

No.

Pause.

Yes.

Yes what?

We got into an argument.

Like what? What kind of argument?

I was poking my nose where it didn't belong. I should've called him to apologize.

What about?

Someone from his past. A woman. Her grave is on Valence Street.

Have I seen Lenny? How long since I spoke to him?

Couple of weeks. At Tipitina's. He was playing with The Closers.

How did he seem?

In what sense?

Did he seem upset? Unstable?

I wouldn't say so. No.

What did we talk about?

Nothing much. It was only for a minute. He was leaving.

Did he mention Ron?

We talked about the show. We talked about his music.

His music.

Yes.

Pause.

He did this. I know that, right?

No, I don't know that.

Of course I do.

Pause.

I don't have any plans to leave town, do I?

No.
I should stick around.
Of course. Yes. Where would I go?

I skip Ron's funeral. I don't own a suit and Willi doesn't want me there.

The leader of the pack issues a video statement. It goes viral. TBNO is not responsible for this one, he says. This is obviously a copycat crime. Authorities should be alert to the possibility of more imitators, knockoffs, false pretenders. It was just a matter of time before something like this happened. It was coming all along.

I drive to Biloxi, build a beer-can fortress on the sand.

I fall asleep. I don't dream.

We're having café au lait and beignets at Café du Monde on Decatur like a couple of tourists on vacation.

"He was a piece of shit," she says.

Her eyes are red. She's been crying, acting like someone who gives a shit. It'll take root if she's not careful, it'll turn into a habit.

"He used people," she says.

"You know better than I do."

She looks at me.

I push the paper napkins toward her.

She grabs them, wipes her nose.

A mime with face paint and a bow tie is twisting balloons on the street corner. Weiner dogs. Hats. Umbrellas. Pink flowers for girls. Blue Uzis for boys.

A young trumpet player on the opposite side of the street has attracted a cluster of tourists. They stand and listen to him play. Couples falling in love. Couples trying to stay in love. Jazz aficionados. Cripples. The blessed and the lost. For a moment they are all here, together, and they all belong.

I spot the man dragging his little girl by the hand. It'll be years from now, but chances are good, the tea leaves and palm lines and the guts of dead animals say yes, yes, she'll tell him one day he's a fucking bastard and a son of a bitch and it'll be the day she fears and longs for most in her life, and when it's over and when the words have been said, nothing will be the same ever again.

Just wait. Just stay alive and hold on.

The trumpet player spins out a series of spiky notes and ends, smiles, bows, wipes his brow with his jacket sleeve.

Coins and singles drop into his bucket.

He tips his hat and the crowd moves on.

He takes it from the top. Same tune, same groove, a loop of notes that flows back into itself. He's making music on a Sunday morning. He's all right. He's got swing.

I check my watch, touch Willi's hand.

She pulls away like I've scorched her.

"Don't."

I look at her.

"When you were little. He did something. Didn't he?"

She looks away.

"Your mother. He gave her money. For what?"

"He wanted to buy back something. He couldn't."

She'll never tell me what, and I don't want to know. The knowing fucks you. The knowing breaks your heart.

I glance around and I'm thinking he's not going to show, I don't know why I thought he would.

But then he's here, standing behind me, telling me he's sorry he's late.

He looks confused. He didn't think there was going to be someone else with me.

He doesn't know what to do with himself, so I tell him.

"Join us, Andy. Sit."

He sits.

"Andy, Willi. Willi, Andy."

They look at each other.

She shakes it quickly and drops it.

He smiles.

She doesn't.

"Nice to meet you," he says.

"Uh-huh."

I push the untouched plate of beignets in front of him.

He shakes his head.

"It's going to go to waste," I say.

He takes one and bites into it. He chews and nods like a child, powdered sugar coating his lips, a tiny white dab of it on his nose.

I'm thinking maybe they'll like each other. I'm thinking sometimes you don't know what you're looking for until it finds you.

She unwraps a lollipop and tucks it in her mouth, removes an envelope from her laptop case and slides across the table.

"You might as well have this."

"What is it?"

"Your work."

"The book?"

"Do with it what you want. I don't care."

I lift the lip of the envelope and look inside. The cover page says it's a work in progress, unfinished, unended, forever stuck in a holding pattern, circling the story and the life it tells.

~~WE DREAM OF WATER~~

~~DREAMING OF WATER~~

PLAYING ON WATER:

THE LIFE AND TIMES OF WALTER "MONGOOSE" JOHNS

She gets up. I see her give Andy a quick look.

"Well," she says. "So long. Happy trails tomorrow."

"Yes," I say. "You too."

She shakes her head.

"I'm staying here."

"I know. It's where you belong."

She turns and walks away.

We watch her cross Decatur and go into the Quarter. We lose her at the same time and turn to each other.

"Want me to order another plate? You still hungry?"

"You're leaving?"

"What do you think? Cute, right?"

"When?"

"I'm going to give you her number. You should call her."

"Where are you going?"

I stuff the last beignet in my mouth. I inhale powdered sugar, cough and wheeze and choke.

Andy slaps me on the back until I swallow, breathe, raise my hand to tell him that's enough, I'm okay, I'm resurrected.

"Andy."

"Yes?"

"Be good to her. She's a good woman."

Windows down, breezy fingers in my hair. The highway long and gray and unspooling before me in the cold morning light. I pull the coat around my ears and drink the gas station coffee. I keep my eyes on the road. I pay attention to the signs.

Jagger on the radio is telling himself he's going to ride those wild wild horses some day. First recorded by Gram Parsons in 1970, before he OD'd on morphine. His friends hijacked his corpse from LAX, got high and drove to Joshua Tree. They laid him in a shallow grave, doused him with gasoline, and struck a match. It's what he wanted, they said. He wanted the road to end out there in the big desert, under the endless open sky.

I rehearse the route, the closest I can come to predicting the future.

I-10 West to Baton Rouge, Lake Charles, Beaumont. Houston. San Antonio. Fort Stockton to Van Horn. El Paso to Las Cruces. Lordsburg and Tucson. North to Phoenix and West again to

Blythe and Palm Springs. Stay on the I-10 and merge onto CA-57 North. Merge onto 120 West. Take Ocean View Boulevard toward Montrose. Turn left onto Ocean View. Turn right on Honolulu. Left on Rosemount, which becomes Roselawn Avenue. Right onto Oak Circle Drive. Park two doors down from the house and kill the engine. Light one more cigarette, suck it down to the butt. Change my mind and turn the ignition key. Sit there, engine idling. Call myself a spineless fuck. Get out and walk to the door. Take a breath. Hold it. Ring the bell.

She'll be happy to see me.

I want her to be happy to see me.

Maybe we can talk. Maybe we can learn to do that again, my mother and I. Why I didn't come to the funeral. Why I live in a drowned city. The names of my rivers. The shapes of my estuaries. The secrets of my floodlines.

Tall order. Take it a down a notch. Put some resentment in there and a shitload of guilt and silent accusations, and I've got two, maybe three days in me.

Saddle up again and ride the Golden State up to Sacramento. Take Exit 522 and merge onto I-80 E. Exit 13 to Virginia St and into downtown. I'll find her. Half the town knows her name by now. She's a local celebrity, a living legend. She has lovers and suitors. There can't be that many dives in Reno.

My phone rings.

I ignore it.

It stops.

Rings again.

I grab it and hold it out the window.

I wait for my hand to drop it.

It doesn't.

I answer it.

"Mr. Petrovich? This is Lori. From Dr. Kusznierewicz's office? I'm sorry for the delay, dear. The lab that does our tests got broken into. It took them this long to get things started up again. You wouldn't believe the mess."

"Lori?"

"Yes, dear?"

"Do you have something to tell me?"

"I wanted to see when it would be a good time for the Doctor to call you. It doesn't have to be now if it's not convenient. Are you driving, dear? Shall I call later?"

"Lori."

"Yes?"

"Do you have something to tell me?"

She's silent.

"Yes," she says. "Yes I do, dear."

Srdjan Smajić was born in 1974 in the Socialist Federative Republic of Yugoslavia. He lives and works in New Orleans. *We Dream of Water* is his first novel.